MITCH A. SCHULTZ
THE WHISPER
THE FIRST BOOK IN THE ANDRE MICHAEL LANSING SERIES

An Andre Michael Lansing Novel

Mitch A. Schultz

ISBN: 9781797050584

Elaine, you showed me how to love again.

Breanna, you showed me joy again.

Brett, you showed me how to laugh again.

Travis, you showed me how to hope again.

The Whisper Reviews

The Whisper cuts deep into the reality of church life and the pain of human suffering. Mitch Schultz challenges us to stop playing religious games and to begin bleeding for Jesus.
—Elaine W. Miller, international speaker and best-selling author of *We All Married Idiots*

One pastor's nightmare begins when a jealous and controlling husband uses his wife to attack their pastor. The abuse escalates as other leaders in the congregation believe her accusation. The pastor's nightmare culminates when the most important person in his life is murdered. The path that brings him healing is marked with the forgiveness and love that he discovers in a most unlikely place. Mitch Schultz has written a compelling novel.
—The Reverend Doctor Dennis R. Maynard, Episkopols.com popular author of *When Sheep Attack!*

Mitch Schultz has written a disturbing story that raises some penetrating questions: If God intentionally allows bad things to happen to good people, why should He be trusted? And, how is it possible that Christ's incarnation, death, and resurrection can help us grapple successfully with the painful and distressing experiences of life? Schultz unwraps the answers to these inquiries in a way that compels the reader to respond personally to the Truth.

—Rev. Peter Nanfelt, former president of the Christian and Missionary Alliance

Andre Michael Lansing: wise pastor, faithful servant, loving husband… but… murderer? What can turn a man from his whole life's purpose and create a monster set on this? Where is God when senseless hate and tragedy combine to destroy all that a man has? Mitch Schultz's novel causes the reader to ask difficult questions with uncomfortable answers. Can God's love really suffice? Can He be trusted? Is there more to faith than the trappings of today's typical church? Join Andre as he is led to a place where only God can save him.
—Brian Mark Duggan, international leader, Latin America/ Caribbean ReachGlobal

If you've been in ministry for any length of time, you've no doubt encountered personal pain and probably experienced severe hurt in your work with the Body of Christ. *The Whisper* points ministry leaders toward healing for the wounds often incurred in the service of our Lord. This book may be just the word you need to begin processing your hurts and find healing for the pain you know all too well.
—Reverend Mark Barnard, president, Blessing Point Ministries, *Mending the Tapestry of Church Life*

Hold onto your seat for a ride that will bring you into an honest evaluation of what you truly believe and why! The heart of ministry is always found in real people crying out to God when all else around them is crumbling. Mitch Schultz tells a story that is worthy of a deep look into your soul. This story will cause you to look for purpose but also help you see the value of the desert places with Almighty God. I will read this book again and would encourage each of you to let this story go into the places of your heart and life that may have shut out God and His ultimate purposes for you. It is truly when we have God alone that we come to realize that He is enough.

—Robert D. Galasso, Alive In Christ Ministries, Inc. www.aliveinchristministries.net

Sacred stillness, deep still waters

Calm the raging storms within my soul

And clear the waters of confusion

As pure and peaceful waters flow

—John Michael Talbot, "Sacred Silence"

And he said, "Go out and stand on the mount before the Lord." And behold, the Lord passed by, and a great and strong wind tore the mountains and broke in pieces the rocks before the Lord, but the Lord was not in the wind. And after the wind an earthquake, but the Lord was not in the earthquake. And after the earthquake a fire, but the Lord was not in the fire. And after the fire the sound of a low whisper. And when Elijah heard it, he wrapped his face in his cloak and went out and stood at the entrance of the cave. And behold, there came a voice to him and said, "What are you doing here, Elijah?"

—1 Kings 19:11–13, The Holy Bible: English Standard Version, 2001

Part One
FEAR

Introduction

People don't really know what they will do in a crisis until they are in one. The true test of integrity is when people end up doing what they said they would do when the time comes to do it. I might boast that I would risk my life to rescue a man who fell on the train track, but video footage from the subways in New York City betrays what most of us are really like when forced to choose between our life and the life of someone else. I faced such a choice, one far more difficult than I ever imagined.

The migraine caused every vein in my head to scream for relief. It felt as though someone else was trapped in my body and, looking for a way out, managed to move an outstretched hand, to grapple past my heart and lungs, press violently past my throat and finally wrap its desperate fingers around my brain—tightening around its circumference. I wanted to join each pulsating vein in the chorus of screams.

The choice lay before me, causing the intensity of my migraine. Would I follow through with the commitment I always boasted of? Or would I run? Would I watch from the platform, or would I be the hero leaping onto the tracks, risking my life for what I knew mattered most? It came to this. It always does.

Chapter 1

I never imagined an innocent conversation, a normal pastoral moment, could turn into this. I loved counseling and excelled at it. Rarely a Sunday passed where I did not stay late at church leaning in on a crying soul. Neither did a week go by when my calendar was not full with one-on-one counseling sessions. Couples at the brink of leaving each other found hope as I urged them to work out their struggles together at the cross of Jesus. Lonely, single men and women found strength in the confidence I offered that they possessed something married couples lacked—the joy of serving without distraction. Even Walt, local police officer and my friend, received my counsel when he and his wife, Charlene, had struggled financially. I kept personal cards thanking me for the help I gave. Walt and Charlene's card stood upright on the edge of my desk just across from where Walt now sat.

"Andre," he cautioned, "this is serious. We don't take situations like this lightly. We can't."

I said nothing.

"Do you know what I'm talking about?"

I looked up, one eyebrow raised slightly to indicate that I wanted him to go on. I had no idea, but I was about to find out.

"Janice Larson and her husband, Whitlock, came to the police department this afternoon. While Whitlock attempted to comfort her through nearly uncontrollable sobs, she blurted out that you inappropriately touched her during a pastoral counseling session yesterday. She also claims this wasn't the first time."

"What?" I yelled, half standing. "What in the world are you talking about?"

Walt seemed shocked by my strong reaction and extended his hand palm up, inviting me to respond. I sat back down, my blood boiling. I knew exactly who he was talking about; her accusation was false. Completely false. As always when counseling, I'd left the office door slightly open, and my secretary knew who was visiting. All according to the rules. I never broke those rules. I applied every possible precaution to make sure nothing like this ever happened. But it was happening. Oh yes, the jaws stretched wide, and I was being pushed right into them.

This was not good.

"This is crazy," I protested, leaning aggressively toward Walt. "Can you please explain what she told you?"

"No, I can't. I can only say that she is bringing charges against you. Nowadays these things usually fall heavily in favor of the victim. I advise you to hire a lawyer." Walt rubbed his eyes. Clearly, this was as painful to him as it was to me. "Look, I know Lewis will work with you. And I'll do all I can, too. But my role as your good friend offers limited value in these circumstances." Walt stood silent for a few seconds, hesitated as if to move back to the seat near me, then abruptly turned and left.

My hands wrapped tightly around my head, fingers gently massaging the most vulnerable areas of my scalp. Walt often visited me in my office. As volunteer chaplain for this small Tennessee mountain town of Lowensville, I spent countless hours with Walt in our professional capacities. Me, sitting in his roving four-wheel office and he in my modest upstairs one. We were good friends; we talked about everything. This time? All business. I'd been confronted. Cornered. As my left hand massaged lower to anticipate the next move of those demons in my head, every word, every movement, every charge replayed in my mind like a scene of failing actors repeating flawed lines over and over.

"Jerk," I muttered. "Just leave me here. Sure, I can handle this on my own, my good friend Walt!"

Sarcasm, my wife often scolded, became my weapon of choice when under pressure. Recently, given the heavy stress in the church, that weapon spent more time in my hands than in my scabbard. Strangely, the anguish and anger welling up inside me rushed a torrent of blood toward the pounding veins in my head. The adrenaline thankfully brought some relief to my migraine, but the pain was replaced with undesirable fear.

I preferred the migraine.

I often imagined how I'd respond if a gunman suddenly approached the pulpit, threatening to kill me. I pictured my head raised, hands outstretched, and my voice firm and in control, proclaiming before all those in the room that I was ready to die. This sort of sacred and noble exit brought a smile to my face whenever I fantasized about dangerous situations.

Not this! This was out of my league. It is one thing to show strength and conviction when faced with the task of defending your faith or saving the life of someone you love. But sexual accusations stick for your whole life. I watched the news enough to know that the mere insinuation of inappropriate behavior left a lasting mark. What's worse, I'm a pastor. Bam! I'm done. Nothing had prepared me for this.

I loved my wife with a deep devotion. What would this do to her? To our marriage? "Oh God," I sobbed. "Why? Why this?"

The phone's ring sounded like an air siren, reawakening every slumbering demon in my head. The migraine returned with a double vengeance, but I managed enough strength to pick up the phone to see what Darlene, my secretary, wanted.

"Dr. Sommeral wants to speak with you," she informed me. The tone of her voice suggested that she'd picked up some clue about my situation from Walt's abrupt departure. At this moment, Dr. Sommeral was probably the only person I could imagine talking to, but I was in no mood for him, either.

"Take a message," I ordered. Darlene, usually compliant, told me I better take the call.

"Hello, Doctor," I sputtered, trying in vain to duck two blows from those demons in my head. "Can I help you?"

"Andre, we need to talk."

I said nothing.

Dr. Sommeral continued. "Pastor, several of my patients today shared rumors circulating about some kind of inappropriate behavior with…"

Normally I modeled composure. I prided myself on taking criticism well. Water off a duck's back, I often said as people marveled at my ability to push aside discomforting murmurings about church leadership or even about me. Years ago, Chuck Swindoll, the famous radio preacher, suggested that every pastor ought to pray for thick skin and a tender heart. I took pride in both, but neither seemed to describe me now. My skin had been stripped, and my heart lay shattered before me.

I slammed the phone on my desk, cursing softly under my breath. Then I grabbed my backpack and stormed out of the office, past Darlene, and toward my car.

Chapter 2

Sophia often pointed out my restlessness. I don't sit in one place long. I find the need to move often. I get bored easily. I blame this restlessness, and the apparent impossibility of settling, on my childhood. Why not? Everyone else does.

I feel stuck between two worlds today because of it. I am jealous when I hear someone describe growing up in the same town and in the same home. Man, they must feel settled. Unrushed. Secure. Me? Every two years I find myself facing the uncontrollable urge to move. This restlessness took me to Kansas as a young man, serving for several years as youth pastor in Sophia's church. Then to Spain for a few years as a missionary. Always moving. Never settling. Why? I believe it's because whenever I began to feel at home as a child, my missionary parents moved back home for a year or relocated to another mission base. Then for nine years, I shuffled back and forth between home and boarding school. As a result, I learned not to settle. I refused to. Why bother?

I never broke this urge to move. Maybe it explains, too, my illogical and irrational sense of relief that change—even through a crisis—provides me. It's my strange paradox. I hated moving, but I needed to move. I never asked for crisis, but in crisis I found peace. It happened when Sophia suffered through brain cancer and when our daughter, Priscilla, died at the hands of a reckless driver in Chicago. These tragedies gave me a cave of escape, an excuse to break from the routine. I don't fear crises; I fear the mundane. I would not call myself a masochist. Tragedies simply give me a place to hide from my own demons; they've become another unwelcome distraction for my restlessness. I fear security. I shun routine and regularity. I needed another crisis.

But not this.

As I drove out of the church parking lot, I thought briefly about going home to Sophia. Then I thought better of it. I was in deep conflict. If I went home, what would she say to me? If I did not go home, what would she think of me?
For the first time in my life, I considered running from a crisis rather than into one. Running from everything and never turning around. I lost my ability to reason, beginning to think irrationally, abandoning every established principle that guided my life. I found myself moving into a fearsome, yet irresistible, unknown, because to return meant facing the people who trusted and loved me.

I found myself leaving Lowensville on the Alcoa Highway, heading north. If I did not stop, I would reach Highway 40, near Knoxville, in several hours. I did not care. Leaving Lowensville, getting as far away as possible, was my only objective. I gripped the steering wheel with one hand and used the other to rub away the last throbs of my migraine as I chose the lesser of two fears, but my choice drove me into a conflict of two realities. Now where did I really belong? Who did I really belong to? This crisis could not grant me safety. It only overwhelmed me with fear.

Chapter 3

The car radio blared Lady Antebellum's "Wish I Was Cold as Stone," drowning out the rushing sound of passing trucks:

> I wish I was cold as stone.
> Then I wouldn't feel afraid.
> Wish I didn't have this heart.
> Then I wouldn't know the sting of the rain.
> I could stand strong and still,
> Watching you walk away.
> I wouldn't hurt like this,
> Or feel so all alone.

I found some solace in these words, imagining a world without feeling, without pain. Without the searing experience of loss, rejection, and, yes, accusation. The song served as an anesthetic, adding to the growing numbness inside me. Shutting me off. Closing me down. I wondered if my reaction was larger than this crisis.

Keeping my eyes fastened on the road, I focused only on my thoughts. Normally I would defend myself against such accusations, not run from them. But these came at a vulnerable time in my life. The pressures of ministry had weakened me. Sophia worried, because I threatened to quit nearly every Sunday afternoon. Just three weeks ago, I packed a suitcase and told Sophia I needed to get away for a few days. I begged her to go with me. She refused. She was relieved when I walked back in the house but not happy when I hurled the suitcase against the wall.

As cars rushed past me on the highway, I knew my response to today's accusation rose from months of tension. I was the board bent under pressure, nearly ready to snap. I was tired of running, tired of one crisis after another. I didn't know if the energy existed for one more. Especially one that hit too close to home. One that would not solicit sympathy but rather disdain.

I neared Knoxville, moving aimlessly along Highway 40. The sight of a wrecked car alerted me that a world other than my own existed around me. The accident seemed to have just happened, smoke pushing angrily out of the bent seams of the hood of the car. The man inside tried to wrestle out of his seat belt. I pulled uncomfortably near the car.

Through the smoke I saw small jets of fire. Soon the whole car would explode in flames. I rushed to help the man inside. The wind blew harder, carrying smoke in my direction. The air felt warm. I looked around for something hard to break the window. Finding nothing, I settled for my shoe. Using the stiff heel, I shattered the window.

"Get me out of here! Please, get me out of here," the man screamed. I moved instinctively. Leaning across him, I searched for the latch to his seat belt, buried in folds of the mangled seat. After jamming my fist through the torn leather, I finally grasped the latch and pushed the release button. The soft click offered relief, but the growing roar of the fire bellowed closer. I leaned back, steeling my muscles to yank the man out. One of his feet caught in the torn flooring but finally came free. With my last reserve of strength, I dragged him a good twenty yards away from the burning car, waiting for the car to explode. It never did.

Both of us gasped for air. The driver appeared to be in his early fifties and looked of Middle Eastern descent, his collar soaked red from the gash on his head. He lay on the ground, and I stood leaning forward, hands pressed on my knees. The sound of distant sirens gave me permission to sit down to gain not only strength but perspective. In a sudden cruel recollection, I focused again on my own circumstances. This distraction had lasted perhaps ten minutes but had now been interrupted by a rush of raw emotion reminding me of my own pending crash.

Now what? I sat with my hands holding my head, the migraine demons eagerly obeying their command to continue tormenting me. When I lifted my head slightly, I saw an EMT place the injured man on an ambulance gurney. I sensed he would survive. A voice behind forced my gaze upward. Next to me stood a police officer, one among many at the scene.

“Are you okay, sir?”

“Huh?” I tried to regain my senses—not just about the accident but about what to do next.

"I said, you okay?" The officer leaned lower.

"I think so," I replied. Fearful of drawing attention to myself, I followed with, "I don't know about that guy, though. Do you think he'll live?"

"Pretty beat up," the officer said, "but they're taking him to St. Matthew's Hospital, one of the best in the state. They'll take good care of him. Right now I'm concerned about you. Are you injured? You're holding your head. Were you in the accident?"

"No," I said. "I stopped right after it happened. I pulled him out."

"Oh, you're the one," replied the officer with a tone of respect. "From what folks tell me, you really risked your life for him. In fact," he pointed toward some trees near the side of the road, "the fellow over there caught the whole thing on video. You breaking into the car and dragging the victim out and all. You're a hero, you know?"

I groaned. A hero? Right. That'll be the talk back home in Lowensville. I pictured the whole town completely consumed with the story of the pastor who…

I did not want to even think about it again. I wanted badly to talk to Sophia, but shortly after leaving, I realized I left my cell phone in my desk drawer. Oh well, I thought, it's probably better. I thought again of the times I came home threatening to run as fast as possible from everything. I bet she relived every conversation now. Every reaction. She knew

I was near my breaking point. Just three months ago, the elders met with me and raised serious questions about the church finances and my leadership style. They never came out and said, "Pastor, numbers are down. People are leaving. There is a growing restlessness in the church—and it's all your fault." But that's what I heard.

"Sir," the officer interrupted my thoughts, "I need a report from you. Let's move over here where it's more comfortable."

An hour later, I wandered back to my car. The late night and the emotional and physical drain from the day made it impossible to keep driving to who-knows-where. Five miles from the accident scene, I took exit 398 and checked into the Slumber Inn. I wondered if I would even make it to the bed before collapsing. I'd brought nothing with me in my sudden exodus. No clothes. No toothbrush. No plans. Fortunately, I had my wallet with the necessary credit cards to pay for the room. At midnight, I closed the curtain, fell on the bed, and disappeared from everything.

Chapter 4

When I was only ten years old, I awoke nearly a mile from the dormitory which had been my home for three years and would continue to be home for the next six.

2:00 a.m.

Dark.

Alone.

Frightened.

With no recollection of how I arrived at the campus generator shed, the loud rattling of pounding pistons startled me awake.

I vividly remember the frightening mile, groping barefoot in the dark, back to my room. Fear. What a strange emotion.

Ever try to draw a picture of fear? Ever try to give it a face or a name? If asked to give a one-sentence definition of fear, what would you write? Ask children to define fear, and they might say, "I'm scared," or "I'm shaking all over," or even, "There's a monster under my bed." Fear is hard to define. Grownups give really fancy definitions of fear, such as the one I remember memorizing in psychology class in college: "An unpleasant emotion caused by the belief that someone or something is dangerous, a threat, or likely to cause pain."

I like the child's definition better.

I don't need to define fear, because I hold its memories. Like the sleepwalking experience. Or two years later, chased by a mad man swinging a machete when my friends and I hiked the river. Or when my dorm parent looked through the window during rest time and caught me messing around in the room. Or the time in junior high when, in a class full of girls, my Sunday school teacher asked me to read a scripture passage, and I read the one in Romans talking about circumcision by mistake! Forget the definitions. I don't need them. I can tell you about fear.

If fear, like the moon, has a bright side to it, I have yet to experience it. Now darkness enveloped me. It is one thing to preach about fear, totally another to be caught in its grip. My sleep that night was interrupted many times, but not because of noise. Not from a knock at the door. Nor the strong light beam that stretched its way into my room. Dread woke me. Fear plunged me deeper toward the endless hole of despair.

I finally rose around 8:00 a.m., more exhausted than when I went bed. I noticed the sign outside my window pointing to the location of St. Matthew's Hospital, probably a quarter of a mile from the hotel. I wondered about the man I rescued. Curiosity turned into concern. As much as I tried to push the feeling away by retreating into the pool of my self-pity, I could not shake it. Ask Sophia, and she'd say that you can take the man out of the pastor, but you cannot take the pastor out of the man. I cared too much. The needs of people drew me away from myself and sometimes, unfortunately, from my time with Sophia. It was a good quality but one I did not always manage well. Even in my most selfish, self-absorbed moments, something deep inside me could produce a ripple of compassion.

A small glimmer of light carried on its beam a subtle ray of hope. It lifted me and, for a moment, caressed my heart beaten by fear. It lasted only a second but long enough to plant in my mind the notion that visiting the man might be a path worth taking. Even the shower that followed washed off enough of the residue of self-pity to make it impossible for me to not at least inquire about the man.

As I checked out of my room and walked the short thirty yards toward my car, my eye caught probably one of the last phone booths left in the country. The simple view of the empty booth and the feel of a couple of quarters in my pocket made me think of Sophia, made me long to talk to her. I was thinking far more clearly now than when I left Lowensville. I knew I'd hurt her by leaving, but I also knew the deeper impulse in her would be to reach out to me. She was like that. We never fought well because she never got as far as putting on the gloves. Instead, her hands would reach toward mine and pull me close, like a clumsy dancer. We would hug and often laugh about the rough way she did this.

The memory made me smile for the first time in twenty-four hours as I rushed to the pay phone.

I fumbled for the quarters, feeling like a nervous teenager in love. My heart beat hard as the phone rang. When I heard her sweet voice on the other end, I began to weep. The weeping turned into nearly inconsolable sobs.

"Andre? Is that you?" I then realized I had not rehearsed what to say. Sophia came to my rescue. "Sweetheart, I know what you're going through." Her soft voice and gentle tone reassured me that what came next would not be a reprimand. "I heard so many things about the counseling sessions with Janice. I don't believe any of it, Andre. But I think the whole town's heard. Even Dr. Sommeral called me."

Her voice grew quiet, as though she'd thought of something else. "Andre," her voice shook. She sounded as if she were about to cry. "Where are you? I'm scared for you. I thought something horrible happened to you. Or…" I knew she could not bring herself to relay her worst fear—that I'd taken my life. I was glad she did not say it.

"Honey," I stammered, wondering where to begin. "I'm so sorry I put you through this, but I was afraid and angry. I acted on impulse. I just ran. I know I need to come home, but what am I coming back to? I'm not sure I've the energy for this, especially after…"

"Sweetheart," she interrupted. "I know. I feel the same way. But I can't go through this alone. Rhonda's supposed to be my best friend, but she won't answer my calls even though I need her right now."

We talked for a half hour, requiring more quarters, and we ended with my promise to head home right away. But I needed to do one more thing before keeping that promise. I would explain to Sophia about the accident and my desire to visit the man. I walked to my car, took a deep breath before turning the key in the ignition, and backed out of the parking space. This would be the beginning of a journey into the unknown. And my fear increased.

Chapter 5

The elderly candy striper at the volunteer desk told me the man I described was in room 522, but she didn't give me his name. I joined several others on a slow journey up five floors on an extremely antiquated elevator. When the doors slid open, I pushed my way past them and paused at the crossing of several halls. Even room numbers pointed me to the hall on my right.

A nurse stood outside room 522 making notations on an iPad. She seemed not to notice as I pushed the door open and entered. The man showed more injuries than I expected. Of course bruises often take time to form and his face was full of them. He looked up at me, and I could tell that he remembered, but he seemed to lack the energy to speak. I stood there for a few moments, feeling no pressure to say anything. I visited hospital rooms often and had grown accustomed to a lack of conversation. Then the man groaned and extended his hand, indicating that he wanted to shake mine. I took his hand, although briefly, and asked how he was doing.

His voice sounded raspy, as if he had not spoken much since his admission, but after clearing his throat several times, the strength I'd heard the night before returned.

"I'm good," he muttered, "but I would be far better if this hadn't happened. How are you?"

The question caught me off-guard, placing me in a defensive mode. However ridiculous it seemed, the way he asked and the way he looked at me made me feel that he knew everything I'd experienced in the past twenty-four hours.

"I'm fine. Thanks for asking, but I'm really more concerned about you. Are you in pain?"

He seemed uninterested in talking about himself. "When you pulled me out last night, I saw fear in your eyes." He gazed steadily at me for several moments. Not a condemning look at all. Rather, I felt vulnerable and exposed. The way he referred to my fear suggested he was worried for me. "Strange, isn't it?" he continued. "I am trapped in my car, everything ready to blow up around me, and you, my rescuer, you're the one afraid."

He offered no reasoning for this twisted, yet penetrating assessment. His continued stare made me increasingly uneasy. What an interesting man, I thought. I took note again that he appeared Arabic, possibly Iranian or Saudi. And while his accent was noticeable, I understood his English.

"Listen," I said, hoping my voice appeared stronger than my insecurity, "I appreciate your concern, but…" The upturn at the corner of his right lip gave way to a slight smile, and I realized he saw through my attempt to dodge his probing. "But you need to appreciate that you almost died last night. Of course approaching the car and rescuing you scared me, but I'm so glad you survived."

"Really?" he said. I wasn't sure if it was a question or an acknowledgment of what I'd just said. He cleared his throat again. "You know, we do all kinds of things for others, and often we do them hoping others will ignore our own anguish. Yes, I see it often."

He coughed, his left hand raised to indicate he had more to say. Once the coughing passed, he cleared his throat and continued. "Selfishness defines our world, but sometimes it comes in the guise of compassion. People help others, go out of their way to give aid, raise money for the poor, rescue animals, raise awareness for AIDS victims, draw attention to sex slavery, but all the while… " He paused, obviously needing to catch his breath.

A nurse came through the door and interrupted us. I stepped to the side to give her space, and as she checked the man's vitals and changed his IV, I found myself staring at my shoes without noticing them. I wondered what he meant when he said, "Sometimes it comes in the guise of compassion." What in the world was this man ranting about, and what was he trying to tell me?

I determined to take control of the conversation when it resumed. A few minutes later, the nurse left, and I stood next to him again. "What's your name?" I asked, surprised by the weakness of my voice. Standing next to someone's bedside always gave me a sense of authority in situations like this. I do not mean at all that I felt superior but that it gave me confidence to look down at someone lying on a bed. I never interpreted this as arrogance or even the desire for reverence. It was something akin to a teacher standing before seated students. It certainly gave me an advantage, one I believe I used as a sturdy platform to offer comfort, encouragement, and even spiritual strength. But here I stood disarmed. "I felt as if I should be on the bed, while this man should be standing over it.

"Before I tell you my name," he said, "can I share where I was going when I crashed?"

"Sure," I said, curious what I might learn. I wanted to understand his earlier comments.

"Ah, thank you, my friend," he said. His speech pattern confirmed he was Middle Eastern. He motioned for me to sit next to him. I complied.

"You notice this accent, no?"

I smiled for the first time. "Yes, of course I do."

"I'm from Iran, but I've lived in Tennessee for ten years now. I was on my way north, to Chicago, to meet with a family member who moved there three weeks ago. I discovered just this past day that they had received some news about my wife and young son who I left behind in Iran." He laid his head back on the pillow and struggled to swallow.

I leaned toward him. "Do you need some water?"

"No, no…just very tired." He forced his head to turn, made eye contact and spoke. "Yes . . . now about my family from Iran." A smile stretched across his bruised face. "I understand they will arrive in just a few days." He rested his head back on the pillow, his eyes now looking toward the ceiling, his voice growing more strained. "You see, I fled Iran. The details are not important right now, but I ran with little planning and little warning, forcing me to leave alone. My life was in serious danger, and if I had stayed, I would have endangered the lives of my wife and my small boy."

When he mentioned his son, his face grew serious, and his eyes saddened. He seemed determined, though, to continue his story. "I lived ten years in a foreign country with few supplies and little to do besides wait. Some kind Americans who served with an amnesty organization took me in, but my staying wore them out, and it certainly wore me out. I had no idea if I would ever return to Iran or ever see my family again. It tormented me so much that one day, about six years ago, I took a train from Knoxville to Chattanooga. I have no idea why. I just needed to move. Bordering on insanity. On that trip, my life changed. It changed not by divine intervention or a dramatic encounter with someone spiritual who offered right answers. It changed at first as a subtle stirring in my heart, which grew into a small whisper, though it never really went beyond that. It did not need to."

"What whisper? What did it say?"

The man coughed several times.

"Ah, but you see, you're asking the wrong question." He looked at me again. "You Americans always need an explanation. You don't settle well with mystery. Rarely content without answers. Oh, this makes you a great nation, but it makes you poor spiritual seekers." He said this last part with a chuckle, hoping, I suspect, not to offend.

"The mere fact that something stirred inside me began the change. That whisper told me I was not in control and did not need to be in control. I did not insist on knowing who had whispered or what was whispered. The fact that this whisper even existed brought me life. Oh, but believe me, I knew the one whispering. I did for years. It's why I fled Iran. He had whispered to me through the scriptures. But there I'd been too busy to listen, too involved in the noble task of protecting others, standing for causes, teaching and mobilizing, training and placing. For me, it took losing and being stripped and encountering fear in order to be still enough to hear again and receive the whisper."

"What do you mean by encountering fear? I mean no disrespect, but I see nothing good in fear. Fear weakens us and clouds our judgment. Fear makes us run and hide." Hearing myself speak reminded me of all that lay ahead and again enveloped me in darkness.

"No, no, my friend," the man said reassuringly. "Yes, you're right when you say fear weakens us and, yes, it often makes us run, but while we think we are running from fear, we are running to something. You cannot run from something without running to something else. You're probably familiar with Jonah in the Christian Bible, no?"

I nodded.

"He thought he was running from God, but in running from God he instead ran into God." His voice turned raspy again. He coughed. Without looking at me, he said, "I need that water now, my friend. Please."

I handed him a small paper cup located at the bedside table. His hands shook as he took it. He adjusted his body to a more comfortable sitting position and moved the shaking cup to his lips for a quick sip. Some water spilled down the side of his face. He did not seem to mind. I gently took the cup from his hand.

He seemed determined to finish his story. "Yes, Jonah. Ah, yes. We were speaking of fear. Fear made him run, but fear also stripped him so completely that by the end he didn't resist. When one of the last layers peeled away, it revealed anger, and this exposed the next layer—a tremendous amount of doubt. But this final layer, pulled back by the one who chased him or caught him, depending on how you see it, introduced him to the one who revealed trust. Not just the quality of trust, but the Being. Trust Himself—the one whom Jonah could trust and should have trusted all along. Yes, you see, fear became his companion, not his enemy. It is when we are truly afraid that we meet Him, but only after we fully face ourselves for who we really are; sinful and corrupt."

We waited a good minute as he struggled through another coughing fit. "Earlier I said that so often we mask our true condition by doing for others. True love happens when we truly fear God. Do you begin to grasp what I'm saying?"

I said nothing.

"You know, I just thought of this." His voice seemed tired, and he appeared to be weakening. "Solomon wrote that the 'Fear of the Lord is the beginning of wisdom.'" He needed what seemed like an hour to gain enough strength to continue. I began to worry about the man but actually less than a minute passed. "I used to read from this that fearing *God* is the beginning of wisdom. Be afraid of the Creator, reverence Him, stand in awe of Him, and you start right. Wisdom begins there. Yet now I wonder if this fear of the Lord invited me to see the blessing from the Lord. I mean by this that fear is something God gives us as a gift. Think about it. Fear keeps me from standing too close to the ledge of a building. Fear keeps us from walking into a dark alley. Fear of terrorists makes us so protective at airports. Fear makes us wise. It's the beginning of wisdom. Yes, I think fear is a gift."

I did not know what to say. I could not even begin to understand how my running from fear would lead me into the arms of Trust. I wondered if I'd masked my true condition all these years. My hidden fear of being exposed and stripped betrayed my life. Was it possible that my love for pastoring and my love for people were really ways of avoiding God? Was I trying in vain to distract God, serving to keep Him from noticing what lay deeper in my heart?

I looked again at the man, about to suggest that what he said baffled me, but the opportunity never came. His eyes were shut but not out of rest. I braced myself by holding tight to the bed railing as tears rushed to my eyes.

I would be the last person on this earth that he would speak to.

Overwhelmed, I did the only thing I knew to do. Trying to hold back the impulse to sob, I pushed the call button. Before the nurse spoke, I informed her that the patient in room 522 had just died. I walked out of the room wondering if I, too, would ever hear the Whisper!

I never knew the man's name, so I gave him one. The name did not seem right, but something about it seemed necessary. As I pressed the elevator button, I whispered softly, "I just met a man by the name of Fear." The Fear of the Lord!

Part Two
ANGER

Chapter 6

I found my car, dropped into the seat, and mindlessly switched on the ignition. I pulled out of the parking space, narrowly missing a rusted-out pickup truck, and began my descent toward a path I preferred to avoid. The only thing keeping me going was Sophia. My eyes misted as I imagined her cleaning the kitchen, something I often found her doing when she was nervous or upset.

Sophia and I met by accident. Literally, an accident. Two lives, disconnected, unknown, and unfamiliar, merged in a mishap. I often thought it strange that for two-thirds of our lives we did not know each other. She grew up a Kansas farm girl, and I, a third-culture jungle boy knowing America only as a spot on the globe.

After we met, I clung to her stories. Her life on the farm, her first love, her sense that she could never please her father, and the tragedy of following the screams that burst through the grain field one morning, leading her to finding him trapped in the large combine harvester's blade. He lived only two days; the impact on Sophia lasted a lifetime. When I heard the story, it was the first time she'd spoken of it to anyone. She trusted me as she dared trust no one before. In her mind, she was giving herself to me by pulling back calloused layers built up by years of sadness. It would be the beginning of Sophia's healing and the start of our relationship. It would take years before she told the story without pausing between sobs. I loved Sophia the moment she opened her heart to reveal this pain and her tender compassion. It would be a place reserved just for me, and right now I longed for her.

The accident that brought us together happened just three months before she shared the story of her father's death. Having grown up in the deep woods of New Guinea, my greatest passion was spear fishing. The love of the sport never left me, and where there was water, the irresistible urge to grab a spear and stab something, anything, became impossible to turn down. Then on one sunny afternoon, I mistook someone's foot in a murky pond at our college campus for a swift-moving fish.

The rush of adrenalin that always accompanied the "grab," as I referred to it, quickly drained out of me the moment I raised my head above the water's surface and witnessed the most gut-wrenching scream I ever heard. It came from a girl I recognized from my philosophy class, whose cute, slightly turtle-shaped lips and bright blue eyes more than once caught my attention. Those eyes now darkened with anger, and her lips were thrown wide open to let out a guttural cry heard clear across the campus. A red stream began to flow through the water. My spear had not thrust into a fish but into this screaming girl's foot.

I pulled the sobbing girl with one hand while holding the spear, still fixed deep in her foot, with the other. Imagine a unicyclist attempting to maintain balance with a strap of his overalls caught and tightening in the spokes of his wheel, and you might be able to capture the scene. A couple lying on the short stretch of beach quickly rushed to our aid as I stumbled the last few steps to a patch of soft grass at the sand's edge. With no time to explain, we placed her in the bed of my pickup truck, and while the couple sat with her, spear now in the hands of the boy, I drove quickly to the hospital, fortunately located just off the edge of the campus. I am sure that was the first time the emergency room accommodated this kind of injury. Several hours later, I visited her in an outpatient room, promising that I would give up spear-fishing for good. I was okay with that. My final catch ranked as the best catch ever.

I grudgingly made the turn back onto Interstate 40 and several miles later turned south onto Alcoa Highway to begin my way home. I had two hours to consider what I would do when I got back. It's interesting how anger can so quickly bully away fear. Across the highway, I passed the location of last night's accident, surprised by how well the scene was cleared. The evidence that something happened there lay deeply seared in my memory. The words of the man I called Fear played in my mind as I gradually increased my speed to fifty-five and pressed the cruise button. I was in no hurry to return home. He spoke of the Whisper. The Whisper that spoke to him, drowning out all the other voices that nearly drove him to madness. I listened for that Whisper but heard nothing.

I'd traveled this road many times before, and in the final stretch, deep in the Smoky Mountains, I loved entering into the first corners of the Dragon's Tail, famous to bikers from across the country but also famous for the Cheoah Dam from which Harrison Ford made his dramatic jump in the movie, *The Fugitive*. Starting at the state line, most of the eleven miles of the Dragon's Tail wound its way into portions of North Carolina, but it ended, conveniently for Sophia and me, several miles from Lowensville, over the border in Tennessee at Tabcat Creek Bridge. I normally lost myself in the spell of the dragon's twists and turns, but this time each turn, each twist, tightened the tension gripping inside of me. Half an hour away from home I was unsure if I wanted time to drag forever or go quickly. No one knew I was coming back, but I still felt a thousand accusing stares piercing the distance between me and Lowensville. When Sophia made this trip with me, she squealed with delight waiting for my traditional tribal-like cry of victory at the Dragon Tail's last turn before we resumed our journey back into Tennessee and toward Lowensville. It was a cry of success, meaning I again spoiled the dragon's futile attempts at making me his next victim.

As I reached this last bend, there were no warrior cries, only a deep, anguished groan that welled from the belly of a man frightened and angry. This time the dragon spewed its fire at me, burning away every last vestige of joy. The heavy realization that my life would never be the same again replaced the usual excitement of coming home.

Chapter 7

A curse word moved uncontested past the usual moral filters that normally kept me from verbalizing what existed in my mind. I felt guilty that I ever wanted to express myself in this way, but the sight of three familiar cars in my driveway left me unwilling to restrain myself. Dr. Sommeral's blue Dodge Avenger, Larry Moore's red convertible, and Sophia's friend Clair's ugly orange VW Beetle warned me that my homecoming would not be quiet. Neither were the choice words that slipped from my lips. I welcomed every angry impulse to ram my car into each of theirs.

The front door burst open, and Sophia rushed toward me. She met me as I stepped out of the car, her arms wrapping tightly around my neck. Her sobs broke my heart. "Andre, make them go away. I can't handle this right now. Andre, please . . . I can't take this."

I grabbed her hand and moved toward the door. Inside, Dr. Sommeral stood near the window while Larry and Clair sat opposite each other on the two armchairs in our living room. Typically dramatic, Clair wiped the corner of her eyes with a tissue. Of the three there, Clair was probably the only one from whom Sophia found any comfort.

I broke the silence. "Do you folks really believe I did something wrong?"

Dr. Sommeral slowly turned toward me, replying with his strong German accent. "I think you know me well enough, Andre, to know I'd not be here if I did not care for you. I prefer not to believe the accusations. How can I? I have no evidence to suggest you did anything wrong. I just want you to know, I'm worried about you. I want to help you."

"Thank you Doctor," I muttered.

"I decided to close my office today and not see any more patients. They seem to want to talk more about this situation than their own ailments. The whole town knows. I can't ignore it and neither can you." Dr. Sommeral sat down on the love seat, placed both hands on his knees and paused for a moment. "I suggest you go to the authorities and tell your side of the story so this doesn't get out of hand. I see no other choice."

"I suggest," I said, raising my voice. "I suggest you go now and leave me with my wife. I haven't had one second alone with her." I tried to control my voice, knowing that these friends had come because they loved us. "Give us some time," I stammered. "I'll call you tomorrow. But please, leave us."

They obliged. Dr. Sommeral looked hurt. Larry said nothing. I knew my reaction hurt him, too. Larry was one of the newest members of the church, and after six months of meeting together each week for Bible study, he made a deep commitment to the Church and I felt at times, an unhealthy commitment to me. He was vulnerable and attached to the attention I gave him. His vision of me as solid and saintly must have crumbled. I thought about extending my hand but suppressed the impulse.

As the last car pulled away, Sophia and I held each other, saying nothing for at least ten minutes. Finally, I explained all that had happened in the last twenty-four hours. I said little about the man I rescued but enough to let her know that something bigger than myself urged me home. We both needed to cling to something bigger, but for now, our energy to know it and sense it had nearly vanished.

I stood up and began to pace around the room. Sophia saw me do this often when relating the frustrations of my day or even when needing to process some difficult situation. This time I stopped and straightened several of the paintings on our living room wall. My favorite painting (whether it hung straight or not, I never cared) was a replica of Fitz Hugh Lane's, *Becalmed off Halfway Rock*, a beautiful painting of three ships drifting quietly in an open ocean with streams of soft beams of light highlighting the edges of the sails. I often stopped my pacing and stared at this painting. I'd always interpreted the picture as the calm after a storm, not before. A storm always settles. No storm ever rages in perpetual endlessness. It sometimes causes destruction, but it always calms in the end. Always. This time, I missed noticing the picture in the frame, caring more about its placement on the wall. I straightened the frame and paced some more.

Sophia ignored all this, lost in her own thoughts. Nervously straightening her skirt above her left knee, she looked up. "You're good at figuring things out for us, Andre, especially after Priscilla died."

This loss, five years ago, left us without children but also drew us to a deeper love, one that, as a pastor who counseled many grieving couples, I rarely saw in others. I always said it was God's proportioning of grace through fire to us. Sophia loved my putting it that way. We cherished this strength, and it became a platform from which we served and helped so many who hurt. We even sensed a call to this wounded church because our own experience of suffering and recovery gave us credibility and opportunity to see corporate healing take place. Now though, instead of healers, we had become victims.

The frame of my life hung crooked, forcing me to again miss the lesson of the painting. I missed the story, because the story remained unfinished. The damage was not complete. The storm had yet to pass. There was no still image to tell of a story of peace following the rage. Sophia interrupted the intensifying monologue taking place in my head.

"What are we going to do about this? What . . . how are we ...I mean, what are we going to do?"

I sat in the recliner, conveniently set in the corner of the room to give me the best view possible of both the window framing the backyard and the TV, for the occasional soccer game. Placing my head back, I flopped my hands down on my knees. "I've no idea, Soph! I guess we've got several choices. We can ignore it and hope it goes away. We can run as far away as we can, but I tried that. Or we can face this, lean on each other, and fight what comes. We'll need to fiercely defend ourselves."

Sophia nodded in agreement. We must stay.

"I think I need to call Jim and meet with the elders tonight."

"I know. Your elders need to stand at the front end of this. I sure hope they support you. Some of our friends surprised me today with their reactions. I'm not sure what to expect from the elders."

I moved to the wall phone and dialed Jim's number. After three rings, I heard Jim's voice on the other end of the line, along with other voices in the background. "Jim?"

"Andre!"

"Are the guys with you?"

Jim sounded somewhat embarrassed. "Yes. I called the elders to an emergency meeting. But I was going to call and see if you'd come over. I just wanted to get our heads around what to do before talking to you. Are you okay?"

I wasn't surprised by Jim's sudden need to check on me. Of all the guys on the elder board, he was the most sensitive and supportive of me, even in some of the more difficult moments. Five years ago, the church celebrated its thirty-fifth anniversary. Just two weeks before that Sunday, the community mourned the death of its pastor, purportedly at the hands of some local youth. I say purportedly because what little evidence existed quickly faded in small town politics. The pastor had achieved near celebrity status in the community, but his life ended at the front end of a pickup truck driven, it was said, by a drunken teenager. Four other teenagers in the bed of the truck encouraging the driver to test the truck's ability to maneuver down the entire length of Main Street's sidewalk rather than the street.

Even the presence of a jogger enjoying a late night run did not deter the gang from cramming a six-foot-wide truck into the three-foot space of the sidewalk. The little I heard suggested that the truck rolled so fast that neither the pastor nor the driver saw what happened. The pastor because he lay dead; the driver because he was too drunk to remember what took place that night. Certain powerful locals forced the matter to disappear. The incident marked the end of a good man but also the end of a good season in the church's history. I was reminded too often that the good days had vanished and heard the ever-so-subtle hints suggesting that I could never replace the dearly departed pastor. This placed me in an impossible situation. Sophia and I took the call to this pastorate at the request of the regional director who insisted that our having lived through loss in Priscilla's death and Sophia's survival of cancer gave us a strong affinity to both the church and the community.

"No, Jim, I'm really not okay."

Switching the phone to my other ear allowed me to whisper to Sophia what Jim had said. "I'm on my way, Jim. Give me about twenty minutes." Ten minutes later, back in my car, I began to imagine the conversation with these men. As I made the first turn off our property, I drove slowly and found myself reflecting on my time in this town. I could not shake the memories of my first conversation with the church patriarch, Pete. Pete, a businessman in the community, was a founder of the church. He and the beloved, departed pastor moved the church from a handful of families meeting in a funeral home to its present state: a three-million-dollar building and a congregation of several hundred families.

People like Pete, regardless of age and health, remain significant through a church's history. If I suggested a Michelangelo, King David-like statue of Pete at the entrance of the church, preferably with clothes on, it would be received with uncontested enthusiasm. One day, following my first visit with a parishioner, Pete knocked on my office door. He sat down, stared long and hard at me, and in a voice reserved only for someone with clout and prestige said, "Pastor, I understand you visited Veronica this past week."

"Yes, indeed I did," I replied enthusiastically. I began to share about the visit, but Pete raised his hand.

"Pastor," his voice became stouter. "Let's establish this right now: Do not visit people in the church, or even in the community, without first letting me know."

I wasn't sure if I'd heard him correctly, so I asked him to repeat himself. The words sounded exactly the same but came with more explanation. "I've been in charge of the Health and Care ministry for this church for twenty-five years. You're not to go behind my back this way again. Do you understand?"

No, I did not understand, so I replied rather defensively, the sarcasm sword again out of its scabbard. "I appreciate all you do. I value it and want you to continue heading up this ministry. But I can't be micromanaged like this."

Pete glared. I continued despite his attempt to intimidate me. "With all due respect, I'll report monthly to the elders about my activities, and you're welcome to request this information, but no, sorry—I cannot do as you ask."

I quickly discovered that Pete ran the church. If he was happy with things, the elders were happy, placing the unpleasant expectation on me to keep Pete happy.

The church steeple pierced the sky a quarter of a mile in front of me. I slowed the car to a crawl, surprised by the anger that surfaced like small knife stabs in an already vulnerable mind. Thinking of my conversation with Pete had not helped. With it came specific memories of other incidents that I'd chosen to ignore or explain away, particularly when Sophia brought them up. Like images reflecting from a projector that refused to turn off, these incidents played rapidly in my mind. Each memory and each thought added greater weight to an already overloaded emotional reservoir. I was somewhat conscious that going into this meeting tightly wound threatened to make me less pliable and less reasonable, but what was reasonable about any of this? Human emotion holds an unbelievable capacity to take in, but it needs a place to spill over. Right now, my spillways seemed blocked.

Chapter 8

The parking space marked "Reserved for the Pastor" mocked me, so I chose to park next to it. Right now I did not feel like anyone's pastor. I hesitated at the front door of the church but forced myself to enter. The conference room located two-thirds of the way down the hall on the main level held a twelve-foot-long mahogany table that reminded me of a Scottish banquet table in a scene from the movie, *Rob Roy*. It seemed completely out of place in this small Southern town. On one side of the table sat four men whom I had struggled to love during these last four years. It seemed odd to me that all four sat on one side of the table with a solitary chair reserved for me on the opposite side. I pulled out the chair to sit, but before completing this task, I looked around at the men one by one, then shook each of their hands. All the men graciously accepted this gesture. I stepped back to my side of the table and sat.

Jim spoke. "Andre, I know this situation is unbelievably hard for you. We've prayed for you, and we want you to know we're struggling, too. We aren't exactly prepared for this sort of thing, but here is where we want to start. Can you explain to us, from your own perspective, what happened the other day with Janice?"

As Jim said this, I recalled that Ned, seated next to Jim and refusing to make eye contact with me, was Janice's uncle. A sinking feeling fell over me as I remembered that not only were there three generations of Janice's family in the church, but I'd been told that if you counted all the relatives in this family, they comprised 20 percent of the church. I had not considered this family connection and its possible implications until now. I felt both outnumbered and overwhelmed.

"Guys, listen, we've talked about this before. We've taken countless measures to make sure no one on staff could ever be accused of misconduct."

Someone had kindly placed a pitcher of water on the table. Before continuing, I poured some in an empty cup in front of me and sipped. "We have windows on doors. We make sure no one is ever in the building alone with someone of the opposite sex. We inform someone else on staff who we're meeting. This makes it nearly impossible for anyone to even hint at inappropriate behavior."

Three men looked at each other approvingly, but their interest specifically centered on the moment in question. I obliged them. "Yes, I met with Janice a few days ago. She shared some personal things with me. I gave some advice. I listened. I gave her a tissue when she cried. I prayed with her, and she left."

Nicholas spoke up next. "I talked to our maintenance man, Brian. He told me that one day he heard giggling coming from your office. He didn't go upstairs, and frankly said he thought nothing of it then, but now he wonders if you were up to something. I always thought we needed a more central place for a pastor's office. And besides that…"

Jim raised the pen resting in his hand and informed Nicholas that they needed to stay on topic.

For the next thirty minutes, I mostly listened to the men talk. Throughout the conversation, my mind wandered from the discussion, a question here and there bringing my attention back to the men but only for moments at a time. I was detaching. It felt like an out-of-body experience. I was looking down at something that included me but was no longer me. People who talk of dying, then coming back to life say they can literally see themselves lying on a bed. They can hear the discussion. They see everything below them. But a different reality forms outside their familiar reality.

Ned said, "We need to protect the church."

Another voice, Nicholas, "We should wait and see how this plays out."

George, who spoke little, commented, "Does the regional director know about this?"

"No," someone else chimed.

"But he needs to know and the sooner, the better," another replied.

The sight of the men standing and moving in my direction jolted me fully back into the room. My body had slipped low into the chair, but now I sat erect. One of the men held a jug of water, the other a towel.

What in the world? I thought. Has it come to water-boarding to get the truth out of me?

Jim put a hand on my shoulder. "Andre, before you arrived, I suggested to the others that we wash your feet as a sign that we are united and desire together to humble ourselves before our God."

I loved this symbolism, but right now it seemed an utterly out-of-place gesture. Given some of the men's earlier comments, which indicated doubt and suspicion, I did not respond well to this idea. I know my body language showed it. Nevertheless, Jim continued. "We do this so that you will receive what we tell you in the best spirit possible."

Too late, I thought. Any humility that existed when I entered the room now switched places with anger. The comment that something needed to be shared following the foot washing caused panic to return, which accompanied my growing anger. Twin emotions, festering deep, took over all my impulses. The command to run and fight grew louder in my mind.

The sight of Ned holding the water jug took me back to an evening conversation just six months after I started pastoring here. Since Priscilla's death, I'd often shared the lessons God taught me through this loss. Sophia struggled the most in these moments because this congregation did not know us during our tragedy. We lacked much needed support. I believed speaking about Priscilla, and speaking about our growth through pain, encouraged others in their struggles. That evening's conversation with Ned changed my perspective. "We've heard enough about your dead girl. It's time to move on." Speechless, I made the decision that night to never publicly refer to Priscilla's death again.

As Ned moved closer now, I felt my chair pulled back, exposing my legs to the circle forming around me and giving me no choice but to oblige. I removed my shoes and socks. George pushed back the heavy table, creating a large enough space for the ritual to take place. Having done this many times during the installation of elders each year, I knew my role. I watched as each man washed my feet and tried hard to appreciate their gesture, but the tension in my heart and the pending hammer blow that I suspected would follow made it very hard to accept this without frustration. When they finished, I sat waiting for one of them to say something. Ned suggested we stay in a circle, so each man grabbed a chair. A few awkward moments of silence followed. Anyone looking through the conference room window would likely be perplexed at the sight of five men sitting in a circle, all but one wearing shoes.

Ned finally broke the strange silence and, mercifully, cut to the chase. "Andre, before you came tonight, we met and agreed strongly that, for your own good, you need to resign from your position as pastor." No doubt the look on my face reflected shock at this announcement. "We feel for the sake of the church, and even for you, this is the best course of action. I'm sorry. The decision was unanimous, and tomorrow we'll discuss with you the terms of your severance. I'm sorry we didn't discuss that tonight."

Still barefoot, I stood up. I wanted to speak against their decision but chose not to. I grabbed my shoes and socks and calmly walked out. I was proud of that part—calmly walking out. I could have done much worse. I heard once of a pastor who, when treated badly and forced to resign, was given one last Sunday to preach and say good-bye. As his parting farewell, he walked to the platform and stopped short of the podium. Then he resolutely turned his back to the congregation, bent low, lowered his pants, and…well, you can figure out the rest.

I possessed enough dignity to walk out of the room and say nothing.

Chapter 9

Sophia and I stayed up late that night, surprisingly calm given the circumstances. She seemed relieved when I told her of the elders' decision to let me go.

"It's one less thing to worry about," she comforted. It's strange. Neither one of us found the desire to pray. We always prayed when faced with uncertain pressures, but I believe anger placed a barrier between me and God. Ever since Priscilla died, my approach and attitude toward prayer changed. I asked a lot less of God than I did before.

The night Sophia and I received the darkest phone call of our lives was the beginning of my disillusionment with prayer—and nearly with God himself had He not shown His sheer kindness to me in the months that followed. Following this tragedy, Sophia often said, "Life stinks, but God is good." It became her mantra, repeated more frequently as a result of difficulties we faced in this new ministry.

Before moving to Lowensville, Sophia and I had a ten-year, productive season of our lives heading up an inner-city food bank in downtown Chicago. During that time, Priscilla's best friend, Darla, invited her to a birthday party. Although reluctant to let our only child be away from us for long, especially in a city like Chicago, we loved Darla and trusted her parents. The sleepover would also give us an opportunity to spend some much needed alone time. After hearing Sophia beg for some "Sophia time," I saw this as an opportune time to give her what she longed for.

Obsessively frugal, Sophia seldom consented to eat out. This made our night out at a chic Italian restaurant in downtown Chicago all the more special. Spiaggia was rated by the famous food critic Steve Dolinksy as one of the top five restaurants in Chicago. The fifty-dollar bottle of wine and the nearly sixty-dollar-a-plate main course made me thankful that Sophia possessed her frugal bent. Otherwise, we would be broke. This was a special night. As long as I was married to Sophia, which I planned to be for the rest of my life, this would be a rare occasion indeed.

The first taste of my seasoned lamb chop, mixed with the accompanying sip of wine, resonated with the sight of Sophia's lovely, relaxed face. Everything told me this would be a night to remember. At first, the light pinging of a cell phone sounded like it came from the table next to us. When no one moved, Sophia laughed, realizing the sound came from the phone in her purse on the floor. She rustled through her bag, took the phone in her hand, and hit the green answer button. She managed to say Hello through a bite of her shrimp scampi. An immediate change came over her demeanor. Working through the second half of my lamb chop, I looked up in time to see Sophia drop her wine glass.

The red liquid splashed on her plate. Some of it landed on the neck of her sweater. Her face turned pale, and her hands trembled. Sophia handed me the phone, too shaken to respond to whoever waited on the other end.

I took over. "Hello?"

"Andre?"

"Yes, this is Andre," I said.

"Andre?" the voice asked again.

"Yes." I managed to reply.

"This is Stanson, Darla's dad. Priscilla's been in an accident. I don't think she . . . What I mean . . . well . . . you should get here right away!"

I asked where "here" was. He told me that Priscilla had been taken to Holy Cross Hospital.

I knew Holy Cross. It was only five miles from our house, but we were in the city. It would take us at least half-an-hour to get there.

"What happened?" I asked, trying to keep fear at bay.

Stanson struggled to answer. "Priscilla was riding Darla's new bike…" He paused, increasing my panic. I gripped the phone tighter, as though urging Stanson to hurry up.

"A car came from nowhere." His voice broke.

Silence.

"The car hit Priscilla."

My head spun. Stanson continued to speak, but little of it registered except that the ambulance, with Priscilla in it, was on its way to the hospital.

I tossed some twenties on the table, grabbed Sophia and ran out of the restaurant, both of us gasping for air. An uncontrollable rush of confusion mixed wildly with desperation, causing my legs to weaken and making the two block run to our car seem like an eternity. A nightmarish cloud hovered over both of us, leaving no time to console each other. How could the best evening ever turn into the worst possible nightmare?

My eyes caught the neon sign of the underground parking garage across the street. We hurried down the steep ramp toward the lower deck. I pressed the remote, pushing the wrong button. The deafening sound of the alarm echoed wildly through the garage. I managed to hit the correct button. The horn stopped. The lock gave the slightest click. I plunged the key into the ignition, all outside sounds drowned out by Sophia screaming for me to hurry.

I did not need urging. I managed to back up and position the front end of my car to the straight path ahead of me and pushed the accelerator hard to the floor. After two quick turns and two more inclines, we surfaced at the closed gate. I pressed the brake, threw the attendant the ticket and a twenty, and yelled, "Keep the change!"

Shaking, I pulled into Holy Cross's Emergency parking lot twenty-five minutes later. Sophia jumped out screaming. Without thinking I pulled into a handicap slot, the first spot I saw.

Sophia met me at the ER door. With her, Darla and her parents. Darla sobbed, her face completely hidden in the folds of her father's shirt. Stanson quickly pointed to the waiting room and said a doctor would meet us when we arrived.

The ER waiting room looked empty. We sat down. After just two minutes, a door marked "Personnel Only" swung open. A middle-aged doctor strode toward us with a somber expression. Across from where Sophia and I sat, magazines littered a table. The doctor brushed several of them aside and sat down. "Are you the parents?"

We nodded.

"I am so sorry. We did all we could, but your daughter did not make it. I am so sorry."

We couldn't dodge this bombshell. A parent's worst nightmare. Yet this was no nightmare. You wake from nightmares. You experience the relief that comes from the gradual realization that everything was just a dream. You shake the cobwebs. Your mind clears. Your senses return, and you move on. But sheer clarity came with this news. And it surprised me. The simplicity of the words seemed almost ridiculously easy. Your life stops. Damage done!

“I'm so sorry. But your daughter was dead on arrival.”

DOA.

Entered on the proper line of the appropriate medical form. In the hospital, it’s noted, filed, and forgotten. In our hearts, it remains forever.

Chapter 10

To say that one recovers from such a loss is misleading. You don't recover. Adjust? Yes . . . but you do not recover. Eventually, in time, you find yourself still alive. You go about your business. You eat. You sleep. Heaviness and grief become your new companions, the invisible, unwelcome friends that you see and feel but no one else does. Others ignore your loss, but you can't.

In the six months that followed Priscilla's tragic death, Sophia and I changed. Not toward each other really but toward others. It did not mean we stopped spending time with friends, but it became obvious that others just did not know what to say to us. We began to withdraw; they began to withdraw. Around the first anniversary of Priscilla's death, Sophia and I began to discuss a change. We were not looking to run from anything but, as Sophia put it, to run to something new.

"I need something different," she told me. "I feel so cramped here in Chicago. I don't get with anyone anymore." I nodded and listened when she spoke like this, until one day we received the phone call that gave us a healthy reason to move on. That phone call led us to Lowensville.

Five years later, Sophia and I now sat in our living room absorbing this latest tragedy in a state of renewed shock. It's not that you can compare sexual accusations and losing your job to the loss of a child, but they are another stripping away, a further exposing of one's true fear—being left with nothing. This spiraling, I later called it, led me to recognize something that lay deep in the cavern of my soul, something that existed before Priscilla's death, that perhaps gained its roots more from my own nature than from any event or experience I ever encountered.

Things that make us angry only expose our true anger; they are not the cause of our anger. But at that moment, I was not ready for this revelation, so I pushed it aside. For a long time, I preferred to use objects to justify my anger. Difficult people placed on my path became convenient excuses to delay what needed to take place in my heart. I was Jonah, running from the Whisper, needing a Nineveh to hate so I wouldn't hate myself.

After the meeting with the elders, Sophia and I, exhausted, slept soundly. Unable to ignore my alarm for the third time the next morning, I forced myself up, quickly made some coffee and sat for a few moments on our back deck overlooking some of the grander peaks of the Smoky Mountains. In the quiet solitude of the morning, I reflected on what I needed to do next. My cell phone on the table next to me chimed a reminder of an appointment scheduled for nine o'clock. A meeting with Dr. Sommeral.

When we moved to Lowensville, I'd prayed for someone I could meet with regularly to talk about life and pray. I wanted someone I could look up to, someone with spiritual maturity and wisdom. I fell in love with Dr. Sommeral immediately.

Following my sermon on the first Sunday, he met me in the lobby after everyone left, shook my hand and expressed his joy in having me there as pastor. "Young man," he said in his thick German accent, "you're God's man for us. I pray for you daily. If you need someone to trust, to just meet with, I want to be that man."

He was that man, and what an encouragement he came to be. His story of growing up in Germany during World War II, his family's arrest and incarceration for hiding Jews in their home, and the subsequent death of the whole family, except for him and his sister, all made a man I longed to both trust and confide in regularly.

I sat for a few minutes, momentarily lost in the sight of several humming birds suckling liquid from the feeder Sophia lovingly provided for them, and organized my mind. Despite his demeanor and comments two days ago, I needed to keep my meeting with Dr. Sommeral. He'd never accused me of anything. He phoned my office and came to my house to show support and express concern. He related what he heard, never himself suggesting that he believed the reports. Yes, I would meet with Dr. Sommeral, but I knew I needed to meet with Walt to anticipate the possible legal implications that came with this charge of sexual misconduct. And I needed to call Ralph Stency, my regional supervisor, though I felt sure he already knew about my situation.

Against every impulse, I made a mental checklist of what I needed to do. First, coffee with Dr. Sommeral, then visit Walt at the police station, then third, phone Dr. Stency. My phone rang, interrupting my planning. "Hello," I answered cautiously.

"It's Dr. Sommeral," said the voice. "We're scheduled for coffee in an hour. Are we still on?" His German accent seemed thicker than usual, and I wondered if it revealed an unconscious tension.

"I'll be there." I said.

I knew I might see familiar people at our favorite coffee spot in town, but I chose to give up any desire to manage this situation.

An hour later, I pulled my car into a slanted parking space in front of Lowensville's Main Street Coffee and Tea. The shop was owned and run by a vivacious thirty-something, single girl from Brooklyn, New York. I never really understood how she ended up in a small mountain town like this, but one thing I did know: she made the most amazing double-shot espresso around. No doubt people in Brooklyn still mourned their loss.

Somewhat fearful, I pushed open the glass door, heard the electronic chime, and cautiously waved to Sandy. She paused from her art of coffee-making long enough to look up and yell, "Hey, Andre. Grab a seat, I know what to bring you."

Seeing Dr. Sommeral's back, I walked to his table, pulled out a chair, sat down, and looked into eyes still filled with compassion and support. He did not extend a hand but gazed at me and spoke quietly.

"Andre, my good friend," he often greeted me that way, and it added to my sense of safety with him. "You're going through the hardest time of your life, perhaps even harder than the death of your dear Priscilla."

A spring of tears welled up and filled my eyes. I looked down for a moment, trying to control the sobbing and simply indicated my agreement to what he just said with a series of rapid nods.

"Son," he tenderly patted my shoulder. I looked up, moved by both the softness of his voice and the gentle touch of his hand. "I must say I'm shocked by the reaction to what remains mere allegation." I began to agree with him, but he interrupted. "Before you say anything, I need to confess that I overreacted. My phone call to you was utterly unangemessen on my part." Noticing my puzzled expression, he smiled. "Inappropriate, I meant to say. Forgive me. Sometimes I unconsciously slip back into German. My friend, it seems this accusation gives people in this small town a reason to rail at you, and I can't put my finger on why. The patients who came into my office spoke as though this were something going on under everyone's noses for months. A few needed this to justify how they already felt about you."

I did not know how to take this. Hearing his supportive comments gave me a slight boost. I knew Dr. Sommeral to be a true advocate who lifted some of the loneliness I feared. The suggestion, however, of underlying feelings preceding this accusation made me uneasy.

In all my years in ministry, starting out as a youth pastor in Sophia's Kansas town, the five years we spent as missionaries in the northwest part of Spain, and the ten years running the food bank ministry in Chicago, Sophia and I rarely experienced opposition. These years were productive years. We seemed well-liked, and our involvement in other people's lives was appreciated. We came to Lowensville confident that our good track record would continue, but of course, the long string of acceptance was now broken. From day one something in the air did not set well with us. The subtle comments, the comparisons, and the expressions of discontent were like apparitions, ghosts felt but not seen. For the first time in all our times together, Dr. Sommeral affirmed this strange tension that hovered in the air of Lowensville.

After Sandy brought my coffee, I invited Dr. Sommeral to say whatever more he needed to say.

"Andre, my friend. I'm trying to rationalize all this. I want so badly to help you, but I sense I need to speak to you about something else. Something needed for your arsenal of weapons in the days ahead." He scratched his head with his left index finger more out of nervousness, it seemed, than to scratch an actual itch. He leaned closer to me. "I need to ask you something first. Please understand, it's only to clear the air so you and I can be unequivocally honest with each other." My silence indicated permission to continue. "Just tell me that these rumors aren't true. I even heard this went on for some months between you and Janice."

My heart sank again in hearing this, but I managed to gain enough strength to tell Dr. Sommeral all I told the elders last night. "I did nothing wrong. I took the necessary precautions as all of us did on staff. Janice came for counseling. I listened. Gave some advice. She cried. I handed her a tissue. We prayed, and she left. End of story."

"I knew this," the doctor replied with noticeable relief in his voice, "but I needed to hear it from you, or perhaps you needed to hear yourself tell it to me."

I nodded in gratitude, appreciative of his kind words. Dr. Sommeral seemed far more relaxed now and continued, as he often did, with a story of his early days in Germany. Another of his World War II stories.

He'd told me this story several times, but I never tired of hearing it. His parents hid Jews. On a number of occasions the Nazis marched down their block, but for some reason when they came to the end of the street to check the row of houses on which the Sommerals lived, they turned back to the block behind the homes. Then they returned across the street on the way back around. This half hour gave the Sommerals enough time to rush the Jewish family across the street to hide in a home already inspected by the soldiers. One day, however, a neighbor who was a Nazi sympathizer turned them in, forcing the entire Sommeral family into a concentration camp in Germany. The doctor choked up as he told of beatings, torture, neglect, and starvation, but today in the coffee shop he said something he'd never told me before. "The hardest memory of those days remains fresh," Dr. Sommeral said. I felt pulled into the story as though I was to experience it with him. He told of the young boy, forced to hold his father down while the soldier used the butt of his rifle to pound on the chest of the nearly dead man. Rather than screaming at the soldier, the young boy, in severe turmoil, instead screamed at his father.

"Die," he yelled. "Just die. Why are you doing this to me? Why did you bring us here? It's your fault. You made us hide those filthy Jews. You forced sister and me to cooperate, but we never wanted to. Just die! Die! Die!"

My cup of coffee froze somewhere between the surface of the table and my mouth, my mind in a state of disbelief as I imagined Dr. Sommeral's agony of having to live with this memory all these years. I wondered if he'd ever shared this with anyone before. Was this his secret pain? Was this what the man in the accident two days ago meant when he said sometimes we do good things to distract God from dealing with what lies true in our hearts? Did he become a doctor with the hope that serving humanity would replace the guilt and make up for the wrong toward his father?

Noting my shock, Dr. Sommeral grabbed a napkin from the dispenser at the side of the table. He wiped away the tears gathering at the edges of his eyes. "Andre, my friend," he said in a shaking voice, "I took all my rage, all the pent up anger of seeing such horror day after day, and placed them unfairly, horribly unfairly, on the wrong person. Worse yet, on the person I loved and respected the most. He did die. While I'm forgiven for this, I can't forget it."

Tears formed at the edges of my eyelids. He was not finished. As he spoke, it became apparent that he shared this because there was something in it he wanted me to hear.

"Anger cannot be helped, but you must manage it." He paused and used the same napkin to wipe away the last remnant of tears. He crumbled the napkin in his hands and placed it under his thigh. I braced myself for the lesson that came with the story. "Anger is a strange emotion, isn't it?"

I said nothing.

"I felt anger toward the soldiers, but I took it out on my father." His eyes moistened again. "Why? Was it fear? Was I afraid if I lashed out at the soldiers they would turn on me? Or were my reasons far deeper than this? What do you think?"

What could I say? I sipped from my cup without taking my eyes off the doctor.

He took his glasses off and wiped the lenses with a new napkin. "You know, after having fifty years to process that question, my conclusion, I think, will shock you. You know the story of Cain and Abel, how Cain's anger led him to kill his brother, Abel." Dr. Sommeral positioned his glasses in place, in no rush to speak. "Do you remember when God came to Cain and warned him that anger crouched at the door of his heart? 'It desires to have you,' God told Cain. 'It desires to have you, but you must master it.' You know the ending of this story. I heard you preach a great sermon on it once."

I smiled weakly. The doctor waited for Sandy to offer more coffee to a young woman seated at the table next to us. Sandy then looked at me, and I showed her my open palm to indicate I did not need more coffee.

Dr. Sommeral's voice softened. I leaned in to hear better. "Anger took Cain and turned him into a murderer. It mastered him rather than him mastering it. It intrigues me, what God tells Cain. The invitation for Cain to master anger meant that God permitted that anger. Anger was, strangely, a gift to Cain, a way for him to learn to love his brother."

Taken by his suggestion of anger as a gift—in the same way the man from the accident referred to fear as a gift—I exclaimed, "What are you getting at?"

"Andre, my good friend. God gave Cain a choice between two things that would result in two different outcomes. If he held anger toward Abel, it would lead to something worse. If anger mastered Cain, it would mean anger would achieve its desire—the death of his brother. Leave anger alone, and you will want the person you're angry at to die. You remember how Jesus in the Sermon on the Mount equated anger with murder?"

I nodded and mindlessly folded the napkin in my hand. I now stared at it, but my attention locked on his words.

"In God's eyes, if you hold anger, you might as well want the person dead. There is no room for love in anger. But God gave Cain another choice. To love Abel. To love Abel would mean to serve him. To master anger would give Cain the desire to love his brother. It's an interesting paradox, isn't it? You can't help being angry, but you can use anger to your advantage. Master it, and you step on its back. And then it becomes a platform to do good."

Dr. Sommeral looked intently at me. "Anger needs an object. It can never be left to itself. In the end, it will cause you to hate yourself or ultimately to hate God. If you hate yourself, you will desire death for yourself. If you hate God, you will want God dead."

This stunned me. I ran my finger across the edge of my cup, the folded napkin sitting next to it. Dr. Sommeral waited for a couple behind him to find their seat. The doctor shifted his chair to make more room for them.

I leaned forward and unconsciously invited Dr. Sommeral to continue as he seemed eager to do. "And this is what baffles me. If Cain had admitted that day that he was angry at God, he would, in the end, have embraced God. Until we admit that we hate God, we will never understand his love because our admission of hate gets to the core of our sinful nature. We are, by nature, angry at God, and he wants us to admit that. Only then can he root it out."

Dr. Sommeral's phone rang. He pulled it out of his pocket and after the customary "Hello" whispered to me that his office was calling, and he needed to take it outside. I needed a few moments to process our conversation. His brief departure provided me that opportunity.

It was strange to me that the more Dr. Sommeral spoke, the more I wanted to run. I respected him. I loved the man. But was he suggesting I possessed no right to my anger? Could my anger really be God's way of getting me to choose love? If I left my anger alone would I eventually want someone dead? Could anger really lead to that? I remembered then the words of the apostle James, "After desire has conceived, it gives birth to sin; and sin, when it is full grown, gives birth to death." I thought about the anger that grew inside of me. Could I contain it?

Two days ago, I'd met a man by the name of Fear. Now I wonder if this appointment had introduced me to a man called Anger. If so, he was not the man I sat across from. He was me.

Part Three
DOUBT

Chapter 11

The coffee shop pulsed with activity around me, fortunately with people I did not know. Sandy was also, thankfully, too busy to talk to me. As Dr. Sommeral continued his conversation on the phone outside, I found myself in the agonizing process of questioning everything about my life.

At thirteen, I suffered clinical depression. I remember waking up sad, going through the day sad, and ending up in bed sad. It worsened daily. Eventually my parents, who lived several hours by single engine airplane from the boarding school, arrived to deal with what the school failed to handle. It turned out that even my parents did not know what to do. I spent the summer of my thirteenth year in Australia undergoing treatment and then homeschooled in the village for the next two years. Two years after that, I ended up in Chattanooga, Tennessee for treatment. Declared cured by my seventeenth birthday, my parents returned to the mission field. I was a new person, a normal person—or as normal as a seventeen-year-old can be.

I'd been fine until I lost Priscilla. Since then, I lived with a constant heaviness of heart. Sophia said little about it, but I knew she saw the change in me. Perhaps she thought mentioning it would delay my recovery. Maybe she identified with my underlying anguish.

I'd hoped moving to the South and taking on the responsibility of pastoring this church in Lowensville would lift me. Both Sophia and I felt a change would help us, but the circumstances here never gave us time or opportunity to see any benefit. Like a community disappointed when their first mall ended construction due to lack of money, we would never know what life in this new place could have been like. We would live in the world of what-ifs. I also found that in this condition, which I chose to refer to as "low-grade depression," my confidence in my faith threatened to diminish. Until Priscilla's death, I never doubted my faith but only because I did not need it to survive. A convenient ritual, a pattern, or way of life—an exercise with others who claimed to believe and love the same thing—but never a challenge. I was never challenged by my faith, and most around me were never challenged by it either.

Sophia noticed it before I did. She dared to bring it up one day. "You're not the same preacher, Andre," she told me. One of the things I loved most about living in Chicago and working for the food bank was the opportunity to preach in a number of local churches. I was enthusiastic, positive, and upbeat. I offered an unapologetic doctrine of hope, suggesting that simply trusting Jesus would sort out the woes of life. I believed it because, up to that point in my life, it had worked. Sophia noticed not that my preaching lacked passion but that the themes became more realistic and earthy. I spoke often of suffering. I spoke honestly about the mysteries of God.

Dr. Sommeral returned and resumed his place across the table from me. I included him in the brief mental processing that had taken place during his absence.

"Dr. Sommeral, may I ask you a question?"

"Fire away, my good friend," he responded.

"I understand what you're saying about anger and how I need to manage it, but you're asking a lot. I've taken two big hits in my life already with Sophia's brain cancer and Priscilla's death, but these existed outside of my control. I could do nothing to prevent them from happening. This current situation is different. It's like I've been thrown into a conspiracy movie. I'm not having a hard time with anger—I am angry. I hear what you're saying, that the anger will drive me insane looking for a person to direct it toward."

Dr. Sommeral nodded and I continued. "What I struggle with is this: a dilemma of faith. I'm not going to call it a crisis of faith. I see it as more of a dilemma. I mean, this has nagged at me for four years now."

"You mean the whole time you've served here?"

I nodded, looking up at him. I waited as Sandy came over to ask if I wanted a refill. Of course I did. Once she left, I continued. "Here's my dilemma: Can you lose confidence in people while maintaining a strong relationship with God? Can both happen? Because right now, I feel one severely affects the other. Can you trust God when you can no longer trust people? Especially if you're a pastor who relies on trust to do your job well?"

Dr. Sommeral appeared distant, as though trying to remember something. He made eye contact again, held my gaze, and with the rhythmic tapping of his finger, he nearly chanted. "Ah yes, to dwell above with saints we love that will be grace and glory. But to live below with saints we know—now, that's another story."

I tried to smile. This seemed a good time to fill Dr. Sommeral in on some of the events that had taken place in the last twenty-four hours. My flight out of town. Running into the accident and rescuing the man. The restless night in the cheap hotel. The very odd conversation with the Iranian and his dramatic last words about the Whisper that rescued him. His last breath in the hospital. What seemed to surprise and, I thought, sadden the doctor most was my meeting with the elders last night, the foot washing, and the call to resign.

"Do you blame me for feeling the way I do?"

He said nothing.

"So, wise sage, how do I keep trusting God when I have lost my trust and confidence in people?"

"Andre, my friend. I want to say so much more, but I don't believe God is ready yet for you to hear the answer. You must discover this answer for yourself. That question will be addressed in time. When you're ready for it. When God is ready for it."

We sat quietly for twenty minutes. Finally I said I needed to go. As I rose, Dr. Sommeral grabbed my arm and looked hard into my eyes. "Andre, don't do anything that will hurt Sophia."

Eight simple words that hung heavy over the room. How could this man know what rushed through my mind? What he said indicated both his concern and also his fear for me. I mumbled something that sounded like, "I won't, don't worry," but my words were weak, and I know my dear friend, Dr. Sommeral, found my response unconvincing.

Chapter 12

Lowensville's police station, located on the east end of Main Street, sat nestled back about thirty yards from the road, allowing just enough space for the imposing presence of a large statue of a Civil War soldier. The soldier stood proudly on a marble platform surrounded by a semicircular one-foot-high wall that served as a convenient place for tired visitors to sit and talk of this historic site. The statue stood in the shadow of a large American flag and a slightly smaller Confederate flag.

The soldier, a local hero, single-handedly pushed back the Union troops, forcing them to ignore this town and move on to more vulnerable areas in the mountains. This story ran consistent with Lowensville's refusal in the decades that followed—and even today—to bend to the expectations of the rest of the nation. Lowensville stood proud on its heritage, and many quietly took pride in its not-so-welcoming attitude toward outsiders.

Several young people, followed by two elderly couples, all obviously tourists, walked past me to view the statue as I quickly made my way to the main doors of the police station. Walt's office was located immediately to the left. I peeked in the window in his door, saw him behind his desk, and heard him tell me to come in before I even knocked. It seemed he expected me.

We had not spoken since Walt first broke the news to me in my office, which meant we needed to get past some of the first awkward moments of this next encounter. I usually hate small talk but found it necessary this time, so after a couple of comments about the weather and Sophia, Walt finally broke the ice. "You holding up okay?"

I responded with my usual bluntness. "No, Walt, I'm not."

"Well, where should we begin then? I know you're full of questions…"

"Yes, I do have questions. Well, really just one question." I sat in the extremely uncomfortable chair next to Walt's desk, the chair he'd previously admitted discouraged visitors from staying long. "What should I expect from Janice? Has she come around again? Is this turning out to be the big deal I think it is?"

Walt sighed, stood up, and walked over to the window. He turned the rod on the blinds to let in more sunlight. He was stalling. There was something he did not want to tell me.

"Come on, Walt, cut the crap." My voice was tense and loud. "Sit down and tell me what you know. And don't hold anything back."

Walt sat down again, and he held nothing back. "Okay, it's bad. Worse than you think. Both Janice and Whitlock were here an hour ago. Your problem is not with Janice. It's Whitlock. He's mad. Really mad. This is no longer about you behaving inappropriately. He's using the word rape, and they came asking about the procedure for filing charges."

"And what is that process?" I was also curious. After all, if forced to face trouble, I wanted to know what to expect.

"I told him that generally you come in and meet with one of our officers and file a complaint. Usually this involves filling out a file of evidence, which involves giving statements to several of us. Ultimately, the district attorney decides whether or not to proceed."

I shook my head in disbelief. "This is ridiculous!"

He ignored my interruption. "There's more. If the DA moves the case forward, then it's up to the grand jury to determine if enough evidence exists to suggest a crime was committed. If so, they determine bail and appoint a prosecutor and on it goes." Walt leaned forward, obviously not finished. "What concerns me most is Whitlock's attitude. I've rarely seen a man so angry. He kept screaming at me, even though I reminded him that I wasn't the one accused of anything."

I thought about thanking Walt but chose not to.

"Andre, do you realize it was Whitlock's nephew who supposedly ran over your predecessor but was never charged? I'm sure you heard stories about Whitlock stonewalling the investigation into that incident. Do you know what this man is capable of?"

I decided not to ask. Some things in this town, like in most of these mountain towns, are not worth trying to understand. The intimidation of the police by local, ordinary people never made sense to me, but I knew the tradition was rooted in long family rivalries and bonds that those from the outside could never explain. The fact that Whitlock could bully the police sufficiently enough to discourage an investigation into the former pastor's death told me a history existed deep below the surface, something that probably stemmed from long before the life of the Civil War soldier portrayed outside the building.

"Whitlock left here screaming, threatening to get back at you for what you had done to his wife. I suggest you call Sophia and make sure she's on guard."

I could not believe my ears. I knew Walt as a good, reliable friend, but this illusion vanished as quickly as light beams coming through a window disappear in the presence of a cloud. Walt was a weak man who cowered under the bully. He had no courage to stand up to Whitlock. I cringed to think Walt suspected Whitlock might hurt Sophia, and yet he had not sent an officer to our house.

My rage reached its boiling point. The sudden presence of fear overwhelmed me. I said nothing to Walt. I left his office and wondered if I would ever again enjoy any kind of friendship with such a spineless, fickle man, the product of a small town rule of law with roots deeper in culture and family connections than in the constitution itself.

On one hand, my ideal of life in a cozy, comfortable tourist town nestled in the quiet mountains began crumbling, but on the other hand, some things began to make sense. I realized that when people came into the church building week after week, it did not necessarily change them. We pastors live with the illusion that if people spend enough time around us, if they invest their lives in the activities of the church and sit under our preaching and teaching, they will become different people. In reality, going to church was only part of their culture, a part of a bigger way of life. People often get involved in church just enough to give themselves and others the impression that they are good people. C. S. Lewis referred to them as people exposed to just enough Christianity to inoculate them against the real thing. Now it made sense to me. I lived in a place where the majority of people received enough of Jesus to keep them from wanting to really know Jesus. And in some tragic way, I'd contributed to that mentality. By serving as the pastor of this prestigious church, I had become part of the problem.

Chapter 13

I jumped into my truck, slammed the door shut, and rammed the key in the ignition. The motor rumbled to life. I grabbed my phone, which I'd retrieved from my office the night before, and hit speed dial for Sophia.

It rang the usual six rings before her voicemail told me to leave a message, and she would get back as soon as possible. Perhaps she did not make it to the phone on time.

I dialed again.

Same thing.

My heart began to race. Oh no! No! No, God, no. My chest felt heavy, and my heart pumped rapidly, as though it desired to match the rhythm of the pistons of the truck engine. My foot hit the floor and pushed the truck forward. I was willing to break the law to get to Sophia. As I hit the straightaway of Highway 32, the speedometer displayed eighty. In a fifty-five mile per hour zone. But I no longer cared. Normally, it takes me fifteen minutes to get home. I was determined to make it in five.

Tires do really squeal when you make rapid turns around bends. I know because I could hear them on the last three sharp turns before spotting my house with its long gravel driveway. The truck barely slowed as I turned into the driveway from the road. About halfway up the drive, I groaned. Two pickup trucks were parked awkwardly near the garage.

"No, no, no!" I screamed, slamming the steering wheel with my fist. Then I swore. I swore that if Whitlock and his friends were inside my home, they would not live to talk about it. I swore if he so much as touched a hair on my wife's head, I would kill him. My anger, fueled by fear, turned to rage. Then I noticed that one of the pickup trucks—not Whitlock's but the other—had a gun rack over its back seat. And the rack was empty!
Frantically, I leaped from the truck.

Nearly slipping on the gravel, I kept my balance and rushed through the garage expecting to make a quick entrance to the kitchen where I hoped Sophia was. Just before pushing the door open, I noticed a shovel leaning against the garage wall. I grabbed it and ran inside. My heart sank as I heard Sophia crying.

"No," she screamed. "Stop it. Stop it. Andre, help! I'm back here!"

A male voice yelled, "Shut up you b—! Just shut up, or we'll end this now. Right here."

I followed the voices, moved by the force of anger that exists only in a moment of rage. But something more grew in me. Something I thought impossible. Not just rage. Not anger. Passion. Commitment. A deep sense of protection.

Love.

A clarity came to my mind, and even now I can dissect every feeling and every thought and every emotion that drove me toward the voices. With each step, I felt empowered by duty, bound by a covenant that swore loyalty to one person—the only person I truly loved.

You do this to my Sophia, and you're dead, I thought. My resolve to defend her did not diminish when I saw her in the middle of the living room on one knee and her hair, that beautiful hair, in the grasp of the lowlife Whitlock. Standing in front of her, a stranger. One of Whitlock's nephews, I assumed.

A bookcase divided the dining room from the living room, and I stopped short of it for protection and time to respond. If needed, I could duck behind the bookshelf. Besides that, I knew this house, and they did not. If necessary, I knew where to run but only if I freed Sophia. I was not going anywhere until she was out of the grasp of that madman and back in my arms.

"Whitlock, you let go of my wife right now," I screamed, "or I will kill you!" I meant every word. "I don't know what's going on here, but this is not the way to handle it."

Still grasping Sophia's hair, and with Sophia now moaning softly, Whitlock pointed his finger in the direction of my voice. "Pastor Lansing—no, I'm just going to call ya Mr. Liar. Mr. Hypocrite. Mr. Wife-stealer. Let me tell you something. No one touches my wife, do ya hear me?" His voice got louder. "Do ya hear me, Pastor? Wife-stealer! No one touches my wife and gets away with it."

"I did not touch…" I got no further.

"You SOB!" Whitlock, so out of control, seemed drunk, which frightened me even more. "Ya pervert! Ya and my wife got a thang going, huh? Haven't you! C'mon, admit it right now, and it'll go easier! Just admit it! I can't guarantee I will let her live, but I'll be easy on you, ya hear? Pastor Cheat, d'ya hear me?"

Oh yes, I heard him. Loud and clear. And I was getting ticked beyond reason. Forget love. Forget turning the other cheek. Jesus did not consider this sort of situation when He said love your enemy and do good to them. Walk the extra mile, give them your tunic. No, the rules changed. This was different.

"Whitlock," my voice calmed. It seemed to scare him. "There is a big misunderstanding here, and I'm willing to talk to you and Janice about this, but this is not the way to handle things.

I didn't touch your wife or do anything else to her. Do you hear me?"

Since this was not a counseling session or even a pastoral intervention, I decided to suspend all commitments to confidentiality. It was a risk, but again, I did not care. Sophia's life was on the line. I had nothing to lose, everything to gain.

"Do you know why your wife came to see me all of those weeks, Whitlock? Do you?"

Whitlock seemed to relax his hold on Sophia for a split-second but then he tightened his hold again.

"Did you know she came because your marriage was crumbling? Did you know she came to me crying for help? Did you know that she suspected you of having an affair?"

Whitlock's face turned red. "Ya got no right, Pastor Cheat, to accuse me of nothin! Besides, you're the pastor, not me. You ain't supposed to have affairs. My life ain't none of your business."

I refused to let go of this strategy. It seemed to be having its desired effect, so I continued. "You beat your wife. Did you know that every time she came to see me, she cried when she told me how you pushed her and hit her and forced her to have sex with you? And you were always drunk. Did you know that's why she came to see me? Who's the cheat? You or me?"

The younger man who'd been standing with the rifle relaxed in his hands suddenly raised the gun and pointed it at me, then at Sophia. "You're crossing a line, Preacher. I wouldn't go no further if I was you."

"Really?" I asked, my voice strong. "By the way, what's your dog in this fight? And who are you? You're one of Whitlock's nephews, aren't you?"

He nodded. "The name's Cleon." He said nothing more, and the look on his face warned me I also better say nothing more. I turned my attention to Sophia, who seemed dazed. "Sophia, hang in there, baby. It's going to be okay, I promise."

But the confidence in my voice faded, and I knew she noticed.

Chapter 14

The scene in my living room seemed frozen in time. Four people locked in a showdown. I felt desperation. These two men did not come to merely threaten Sophia. I was their target. I realized I owned little time to act. Not sure how this would change anything, I asked Whitlock to call Walt. Perhaps he could help us sort this out. I began to move for the cell phone in my back pocket, a move Whitlock's nephew apparently did not want me to make.

"Don't you dare reach for any gun, Preacher," he screamed.

Exasperated, I replied. "I'm not getting my gun. I don't even own a gun. I'm simply suggesting that we call Walt to help us through this."

Whitlock yanked harder at Sophia's hair, and the expression on her face told me she had lost all will to fight. "Walt ain't got nothin' to do with this, liar man," Whitlock said. "This is between me and you, understood?"

Something in me snapped. My hand moved slightly toward the shovel resting behind the bookshelf. Anger became my adrenaline as I grabbed the shovel, raised it, and lunged toward Whitlock. At least the broken jaw bone and large laceration on the left side of his head led the police to believe I did this. I only recall the loud cracking sound. And when the echo subsided, Sophia's body slumping on the ground, a pool of blood spilling from the side of her head.

My Sophia. The one thread holding the worn tapestry of my life together. Ripped out in a senseless moment.

Sophia.

Gone.

Chapter 15

I have no memory of what I did next, but I was told later that I fell to the ground and wailed for a long time. Whitlock and the nephew fled the scene, certainly hoping to hide behind their own tribal law once again. However, they'd crossed an unexpected red line. Overwhelmed by my loss, I did not ask the details of their arrest. I would find out soon enough.

In the meantime, I faced the agonizing responsibility of forcing myself to adjust to Sophia's death. I remember little of that night. I knew the house bustled with activity as several policemen came and went. I wept uncontrollably again when Samuel Gruber from Lowensville's funeral home arrived with Mick and Ted to remove Sophia's body. Samuel approached me. When I looked up, I saw tears in his eyes.

"Andre, I have no words. No words at all." His arm around my shoulder shook with me.

"Thank you," I muttered.

"As hard as this is for you to hear," he said, "I'll call you tomorrow and make arrangements."

"Yes. Yes, thank you, Sam," I said between sobs.

Everything from that night remained a blur. I was the frozen image in a room bursting with movement. Dr. Sommeral arrived. Walt had called him. He rushed to my house. He sat with me but said little. Before he left, he promised to be back in the morning.

Strangely, I slept soundly. The pounding knock on the door woke me and with it all the memories from the day before returned to taunt me. I struggled out of bed and moved down the hallway as the knocking persisted. I forced myself not to look at the spot of Sophia's last moments. Stumbling through the foyer, I steadied myself against the bookshelf, fighting off the memory of standing in that place as Sophia screamed for me to help her. I rushed past but could not shake off the image of her helpless body in the hands of Whitlock. By the time I reached the door, I was exhausted.

Dr. Sommeral helped himself in, and after closing the door, he took me in his arms and held me. He pulled back and looked at me through eyes soaked in tears. He began to speak but then chose not to. We walked to the dining room and sat down. Neither of us spoke for a long time until I broke the silence.

"Dr. Sommeral," I said, surprisingly composed. "I have a lot to do today. Will you help me?"

"Oh, yes, of course. It's why I'm here. How may I help?"

I choked. "The last thing I want to do is plan a funeral."

"I can only imagine," Dr. Sommeral said with deep sympathy. "I'm so sorry."

"Everything leading up to this seems meaningless," I said. My mouth felt dry. I walked to the kitchen, grabbed a glass, filled it with water and sat back down. "I'm sorry. Did you want some water?"

Dr. Sommeral's hand touched my arm. "I'm good," he said with a gentle smile.

"I need strength to go through this, Doctor. But I'm scared of what comes next. The concern about Janice's accusations will diminish when everyone finds out what Whitlock did. I got enough out of the madness last night to conclude that he masterminded Janice's allegations."

Dr. Sommeral took a cup holder from the table and turned it mindlessly in his hands. "Yes, I wondered about that. But…"

"No, let me finish. Right now I must focus on Sophia." I was surprised by the calmness in my voice but more surprised by the coldness in my heart. "Will you help me with the funeral arrangements? I mean, will you go with me to the funeral home and plan things out? Today?"

"Andre, my dear friend. Of course I will. Tell you what, why don't you shower and get dressed, and we will go, okay?"

An hour later we were in the car. Two hours later, plans were made for a funeral on Saturday. On the way home, Dr. Sommeral received a call from Walt that Whitlock and the nephew, Cleon, had been arrested for Sophia's murder. When Dr. Sommeral told me, my anger welled to a rage. I wanted them to hurt.

We held the funeral service but kept it very private. Sophia's mom flew in from Kansas. Dr. Sommeral attended, along with several close friends made during our four-year ministry. I am sure our supervisor, Dr. Stency, tried to contact me, but I had thrown away my phone. I doubted he would visit since he rarely travelled. I was fine with that.

Whitlock's arrest meant Janice was no longer intimidated by her husband. Later, in a sincere act of remorse, she confessed to the police that Whitlock coerced her to make up the rape charges. He suspected his wife was infatuated with me, which explained his anger and actions toward Sophia and me. Why Whitlock went to this extreme, knowing the charges were made up, confounded me. The elders tried to reconcile, but I refused to meet with them. I did take one opportunity, several weeks after Sophia's death, to say good-bye to the congregation in a five-minute disjointed statement. Many cried but some remained indifferent. And a few were more than happy to see me leave.

Dr. Sommeral met with me several more times, but a week after Sophia's death, I started to ignore the knocks on the door and the German accent calling my name. I began to drink and abused the oxycodone given to help my migraines. I used both to pretend that nothing had happened. Walt told me the trial for both men would be months away. I did not care. I knew I would have to testify against Whitlock and the nephew, Cleon, but at the moment, all I cared about was retaining my sanity.

I fell fast, and no hand reached out to grab mine.

Chapter 16

When you hurt and you are alone, you hurt alone. The choice to remove yourself from everyone around you places you in isolation. Many made multiple attempts to reach out to me, but I'd closed down. Those who managed to get past my front door or who happened to reach me outside by the pond all, with time, gave up.

I became a recluse. I shut down so much that I hold little memory of what I did and how I managed in those months. Never heavy, I lost fifty pounds. My beard grew long. My hair, also long, remained unwashed. I ate little, watched no TV, and rarely left my property.

A letter showed up in the mail one day with a date for a trial. It informed me I would be contacted to testify and that I would be contacted by the prosecutor, Simeon Davis, to discuss the case. The date was still months away. In a twisted way, the letter gave me something to look forward to. It lifted me enough to want to move past my grief. I longed not for closure but for revenge. I wanted the men who took my wife's life to hurt for what they did, and the desire to inflict pain remained the singular strand of my existence.

One morning, in an unusual moment of sanity, I lay in bed and allowed myself to think about Sophia for the first time since she'd died. I would never forget her, but I had not permitted myself to think of her. When I had allowed it, what I saw was not the beautiful, bouncing love of my life whose smile melted me. When I thought of Sophia, the image that came to mind was a slumped body lying on our living room floor in a pool of blood. As long as this was the image my mind conjured, I refused to think of her.

But that morning, something began to change. The ceiling fan provided the perfect amount of air to chase off the sweat that had gathered during a brief walk around the pond. Absently, I began to remember Sophia before her death. Conversations from several months before the false accusations at church replayed in my mind. I allowed myself a brief smile as I thought about the hike we'd taken a year ago, picking up a portion of the Appalachian Trail one mile from our house. Frugal Sophia never bought new shoes. Every hike we'd been on since we met, her feet were supported by the same pair of Nike tennis shoes. She must have held some kind of a world record for the shoe with the most miles. But I doubt anyone cared.

We left early that morning, planning on a good five-mile hike into the forest and the five miles back. About four miles into the hike, Sophia's right foot caught a root. The root held firm. Her shoe did not. Walking behind her, I saw the whole thing and later enjoyed teasing her with a play-by-play of what happened. The shoe came apart at the arch, ripping off the top of the shoe and somehow managing to also tear off the heel. Sophia refused to be outmaneuvered by a stubborn root. She would not give up on those shoes. She asked for my pocketknife, tore off a foot-long piece of the offending root, and used it to tie a temporary wrap around her shoe. It lasted until we got home.

It was a tough decision for Sophia, but she finally agreed that the shoes needed to retire for good. They now hung on a nail in our bedroom. As I looked at them for the first time in months, I laughed. Not a long laugh or a deep laugh. It did not lift me out of my fog nor did it distract me for long from my misery. Yet I laughed. And while I refused to acknowledge it right then, I later looked at that moment as a small fracture line that threatened to disturb my wallowing insanity.

Weeks went by, and I changed little. The occasional run to the gas station for beer and milk and several other staple items. Walks around the pond. Sitting long hours on the deck. Those were the only activities that kept me moving. I lost track of time. I ran inside when I saw people approach my driveway. I ignored the knocks on my door.

One afternoon, I walked aimlessly into the bedroom and noticed a booklet on the floor near Sophia's bookshelf, on her side of the bed. I picked it up and turned it over.

Sophia's journal.

I grabbed a beer, walked out to the deck, set my feet up on the footstool. I set the beer on the coffee table and for a moment, just stared at the front of the journal which held a laminated pressed flower. I recognized it now as having come from a rose bush at the southern side of our house. Sophia planted that bush shortly after we moved in and often told me it helped her in her grief over Priscilla's death. It meant a lot to her. Now it meant a lot to me.

Sophia often wrote in this journal, more often in the months before her death. The thought of reading it never crossed my mind before.

Now, I held it as memories of Sophia's death flooded in, threatening to drown me. At Sophia's funeral, several friends suggested that at least we could protect our memories of her. I read a book written by a pastor who lost his son to brain cancer shortly after his wife suffered cancer, and I identified with his cynicism regarding the overly easy things people say in loss. He especially struggled with this idea that memories of lost ones are comforting. After reading his story, I felt admonished and tried to carefully choose my words when speaking to people who grieved. The author had said that the memories of someone we love, now dead, are more tormenting than comforting. For that reason, I found myself afraid to open Sophia's journal. Up to this point, I had preferred to not think of her.

The pressed rose on the front of the journal urged me to open and read. I obeyed. Not sure where to start, I turned to the back page and noticed an entry written the morning she died. I allowed the pages and pages of entries to rush through my fingers. Most entries appeared brief, perhaps five or six lines. I went back to the final entry and decided to start there.

April 13—I woke up this morning afraid for Andre. He has some hard discussions coming with Dr. Sommeral and Walt and Dr. Stency. I prayed for him this morning, for courage and patience and that he not give up. I don't know how I should be with him. We are both hurting, and I'm not sure who's stronger right now. We need each other, but neither of us can help the other. We are weakened by our weakness, grasping and reaching but lacking.

The previous entry pierced like a sharp knife in my heart. She had written it the day I disappeared.

April 12—Our world is collapsing. Andre faces problems at church. He is gone. No idea where he went. Tried to call him, but he is not answering his phone. Rumors are spreading about Janice, but I know Andre. Good gracious! Andre having an affair? No way! My husband is so godly. He is so good. I trust this man! The whole world could be convinced that he was unfaithful, but I know him. I know him, and I love him. I know he left to get his bearings. I know he struggles dealing the right way with things. Besides, this is just one more heartache added to a lot of others. I'm worried about him, but at the same time I trust him and know he'll not do anything stupid.

Her next statement stunned me.

I took time this morning to ask God to place something or someone in Andre's path to keep him from doing anything stupid. After I prayed, I felt an eerie and overwhelming sense that God intervened.

She apparently forgot to mention this when I told her about the man called Fear. Had God orchestrated all that to stop me? Did He work that way?

I flipped back and found an entry from a year ago, the day several women from the church approached Sophia asking why she was not more involved in the women's group. I was surprised by this entry, because she never complained about the confrontation but simply told me it happened.

October 3—(A Bad Day) Sally, Rachel, and Karen took me out for lunch today. I was excited because I was beginning to wonder if I could ever make friends here. It was a disaster. When we sat for lunch, Sally asked me why I was not attending the weekly women's Bible study. Rachel told me I was a bad example to the rest of the women. As a pastor's wife, I should take the lead. Karen said nothing. I prayed for them as they talked to me, that Jesus would give me a love for them despite what they asked of me. I guess I could have told them that I do tutoring at the local school with special needs kids at the same time as their Bible study, but I did not feel the need to defend myself. God defends me. Besides, their attitude does not seem very right to me, and I sensed that whatever I said won't make a difference. A spirit of contention seeks until it finds a reason to accuse, and when none exists, more rocks are turned until something is found. If I had defended myself and explained why I was not at their Bible study, they'd find something else to criticize. I know whom I serve and am content with that.

"Oh Sophia." I cried for the first time since the day Sophia died. The meltdown in the living room the moment of her death had emptied me of tears. I had nothing left. But, oh, I cried now. I wept because Sophia's godliness made me feel ugly. I hadn't measured up to her. How could I? She told me about meeting with these women but did so in such a way that I had no clue they had hurt her this badly.

After my tears had spent themselves, I found the entry written just two weeks after Priscilla's death. It was the first evidence that Sophia harbored any anger.

August 22—I'm racked with irretrievable anger. I'm scared that this anger might turn into bitterness, and this bitterness will turn into vengeance, and this vengeance will turn into action toward the man who took Priscilla's life. I want him to hurt. I want him to die. Yesterday I searched the web looking for more information about him. I've done this every night for the past week while Andre sleeps. I do not want him to see this part of me. I want to hurt this man. I want to hurt his family. I found his address—63 South Fox Avenue, South Deering, Chicago IL— but I'm not sure what I'll do with it.

I kept the journal open on my lap, sipped my beer, and allowed my mind to return to that painful time in our lives. I was afraid to because I did not want its memory to magnify the travesty of Sophia's death. I was afraid of being tormented again. But I could not believe Sophia felt vengeful.

It suddenly struck me that I never held any anger toward the man. I remember his arrest and sentencing—something like six months in jail. Mildly drunk, he was cited for reckless driving, not for intoxication. This apparently enraged Sophia, and I never knew it. Where did she place this pain? She either overcame it or contained it well. I wondered what she had considered doing to the man. What frightened me more? Perhaps she had done something no one had found out.

No, not Sophia. I would have seen evidence of such a crime.

At the very end of this entry, about three lines down as though she wrote it later in the day, four small syllables seemed to form one word. I looked at the word, repeated it several times slowly.

te-te-le-stai!

It was not English. After reading it over several times, it came to me. The syllables were Greek. One word that spoke of redemption. Of sacrifice and freedom. I knew the word well. Translated into English it meant three words: paid in full. One word that prevented Sophia from holding on to anger for more than two weeks. Godly Sophia, drawing from a deep belief in something greater than herself, something that outweighed her loss, replaced her anger with love. This word made it possible for Sophia to discard all her anger. In these words she heard the cry of Jesus from the cross: It is finished.

These words, this cry, had washed over her, cleansing and restoring her shattered heart. It explained her life. She was a godly woman, such a godly woman. I found myself angry at her. She had given up her hate, throwing it away for a faith I had concluded did not work. I threw my beer can hard against the deck but found no relief. I had lost my trust in people, and as I feared, that had caused me to lose my trust in God.

God crossed a line when He took Sophia. He'd gone too far. I refused to come back to Him. I no longer believed in Him. You cannot return to something that does not exist.

I wanted to toss the journal over the deck and into the pond, but having just read Sophia's words, it seemed she was in the room with me. I could not discard her thoughts with her watching. Again, I contained my anger.

But her words entertained me further. I had not yet reached my end. To me, the matter was not paid in full. Sophia's entry woke something in me, but it would not lead to godliness. Something stirred within, but it was not love. Love was absent. Hate ruled.

When Priscilla died, I didn't allow myself to feel anger. How could a pastor stand in front of people in a church in Chicago or in Lowensville, Tennessee and harbor hate? Could he get away with it? Of course not! I pushed the anger down, using my spiritual facade as a tool to drive it down deep. I could not hold anger, because pastors were not allowed to be angry.

Now the props had been taken away. No longer a pastor, I was without excuse. I had wasted four years trying to deny what I knew truly existed inside me. The matter was not paid in full. Sophia was wrong.

Her mantra—faith, hope, and love—stood in contrast to mine—fear, anger, and now a new emotion, the desire for revenge. I felt no confidence in what Sophia's God did for her. This was only the beginning. I had some settling to do and, unbeknownst to me, so did the One I was running from.

Part Four
TRUST

Chapter 17

Had I not read Sophia's entry about the man who killed Priscilla, I would not have taken the course of action I did. I realized now, I had simply managed my anger toward the man. I had contained it. Covered it by giving myself to those I served. Hate lingered, waiting for the right time to surface. As weeks passed, I took time to think. Time to remember. I revisited often the tragedy of Priscilla's senseless death. My desire to hurt the man who caused that death increased each day. Whitlock and his nephew were in prison, so I couldn't harm them. So I deflected my anger toward the other man who took from me. I did nothing to stop these thoughts. They obsessed me as I journeyed into madness.

Three months following Sophia's death, Simeon Davis, the prosecutor assigned to the cases against both Whitlock and Cleon, called and asked when we could meet. With nothing else to do, I suggested he come by the next day. I chose to shut myself off from everyone else I knew but welcomed this man who served well my obsession for revenge.

I had never met Simeon Davis before. He sat across from me in my kitchen, dressed impeccably in a three-piece, steel-gray suit, in control and cool even on a hot July day, his impassive eyes fixed on me.

"First," his cultured voice intoned, as I expected from a prosecutor, "let me say, Pastor Lansing, my heart breaks for your loss. Words are not sufficient and will never be sufficient. A tragic event."

I nodded a thank you.

"As you know, both Mr. Whitlock Larson and his nephew, Cleon, sit in prison awaiting trial."

"Yes. I understand that bail was denied, right?"

"Oh, yes indeed. The judge never considered anything else. But…"
I looked up with a start, wondering what would come next.

"Don't worry, Pastor. We expect this in a mountain community like Lowensville. Whitlock Larson is very well-known in this town."

"I'm fully aware of that." I knew what was coming and chose to speak for Simeon. "An impartial jury will be hard to find here, right?"

"Yes, indeed. Very hard." The prosecutor's voice lowered nearly to a whisper, yet each word remained clearly audible. He pushed his chair back, walked to the window, and stared at the large oak tree forty feet from the back of our house. Two squirrels chased each other on several of the lower branches. Simeon turned slowly, leaning down toward the table and placing both palms on the surface. His voice took on a less professional tone. As he relaxed, I heard more of the local accent previously hidden by his official role.

"Pastor, I don't give a darn where the trial is held. We'll nail these murderers come hell or high water. I promise you that."

I believed him and let the anger take over another part of my heart. Again, I thought of Priscilla's killer and imagined all three men on trial. The thought soothed me. I was the jury and the judge. I condemned all three to hell.

Simeon interrupted my thoughts by pulling back his chair and sitting down again. His eyes bored deep into mine, and I felt that he read my thoughts. "I'll not rest. Do you hear me?"

I nodded.

"It could take four to six months to set the venue and get the jury selected. You may travel or stay here, but we need to keep in touch. In fact, let's do this. I'll call you every Monday and apprise you of our progress."

I nodded. We stood and shook hands. I walked him to the door, closed it behind him, and stood in the hallway for a very long time. Lost in my thoughts. Fed by my thoughts. Left alone with time. Plenty of time. And the assurance that the two men who took Sophia from me awaited their day in hell.

And yes, time to consider another man who had yet to pay for what he had taken from me.

The next day, I decided to follow the impulse to seek out that man and carry out what for these years had remained unfinished. I needed to travel to Chicago. I called Simeon and told him I was leaving town in a few days.

A week later, I found myself in my red 2000 BMW 323i heading back up Interstate 40, hoping to arrive in Chicago in less than twelve hours. Compelled by a mission, one Sophia foolishly traded for a conviction of faith, my job was to finish what she failed to undertake. I owned her mislaid mission. I was doing this as much for Sophia as I was for myself and even for Priscilla. I no longer saw Dr. Sommeral's words that anger would end in death as a warning. Now anger was a motivation. I was driven by it, and there was only one way to rid myself of it. It became my master, and I stood ready to obey its demand for vengeance.

Anger needed its object. So I headed north.

I tried in vain to shake off what happened the last time I left town. I cringed when I neared the site of the accident of the man called Fear. But an invisible force pulled me toward the place, the impulse to speed up increasing the tension, similar to two magnets repelled by matching polar fields. I broke through only to sense another force field several miles later at Saint Mathew's Hospital. As happened last time, the urge to stop there overruled the desire to keep driving.

At first I ignored the pull of the place, but the irresistible impulse that lay in this shepherd's heart was not yet completely overrun by self-pity and impending insanity. I did not need to know how the man was doing. He had died. But I could not shake away his story. Like a high voltage light turned to eyes accustomed to the dark, something flashed on in my mind. The man called Fear had been traveling to Chicago for information from relatives about his wife and child in Iran. And I, too, was on my way to Chicago.

I tried to push away the voice that urged me to stop. I wanted to keep driving. I wanted to stay focused, to not allow anything to interfere with this mission. The voice persisted. Voices that speak to you from within are unwelcome voices. You cannot walk away from them. Neither can you tune them out. I had two choices: keep driving and let the voices drive me mad or obey them and then resume my mission. Against my will, I chose the latter.

I parked my car in a ten-minute parking space and approached the hospital entrance. Unsure where to begin, I asked where I could find information about a patient who had died here four months before. The candy striper paused from her crossword puzzle and pointed down the hall to a room marked Administration. I thanked her and walked slowly toward the door, unsure how they would cooperate with a stranger requesting information. This was not permissible by HIPPA regulations. Then I had an idea. Surely they remembered the story of the hero who pulled the man out of a burning car. Yes, it was sad he died, but it did not diminish the heroic action of the unnamed stranger. Now the hero decided to take off his mask and show up. Surely this would work.

The plaque on her desk read, Cynthia Haverson. Her position, Hospital Administrator.

"Great to see you, Cynthia." I added animation to my voice.

"Great to see you, too," she smiled.

"Hey, listen. You might remember this since I know it was in the newspaper, but several months ago an accident happened on the highway, and an Iranian man trapped in his car was rescued. Do you remember that?"

"Oh, we all remember that."

"My name is Andre Lansing, and I'm the man who rescued him."

"That's amazing." She stood and reached for my hand.

I feigned a look of humility. "Unfortunately, I was not able to stay when all that unfolded. Needed to rush out of town. I had an important conference to attend."

"I see," she said encouragingly while moving toward the door.

"Yup." I wondered how far to go with this made-up story. "I had to rush out of town because of the conference. In fact, I was running late, and the keynote speaker should never be late, particularly while three-thousand church delegates wait."

Cynthia waited, but I could tell she was impatient. She wanted to run somewhere. The moment I finished, she exclaimed, "Stay here, Mr. Lansing. Several people will want to meet you."

When ten minutes passed, Cynthia rushed back into the room with four other people. "Mr., Lansing, I want you to meet the doctor assigned to Dr. Sami Firouz during his brief stay in the hospital." She smiled again. "May I introduce you to Dr. Jamison?"

I shook hands with the doctor and then with the three nurses who had cared for Dr. Firouz. This was way too easy. They begged me to explain what happened that night. The local paper ran the story but didn't know my name because I had left town, making the whole incident even more mysterious and dramatic.

For a moment, I knew what it was like for the President of the United States to read a children's book to the wide-eyed gaze and gawking mouths of elementary students. Of course I embellished the story. I even envisioned myself wearing a red and blue suit with a big S covering the front of my shirt as I wove the yarn. Finally realizing they needed to return to work, each shook my hand and exited the room, leaving me alone with Cynthia.

Completely aware that I exploited her misdirected adulation, I put the bait on the hook and threw in the line. "You know, Cynthia, I was just thinking—and man, I can't believe I didn't think of this until today. Do you happen to have contact information for Dr. Firouz? I remember when I visited briefly, he said something about heading to Chicago and that happens to be where I'm going now." Sensing her eager response, I let the line out just a bit more. "It'd be awesome if I could contact his next of kin."

Cynthia seemed almost too eager. She took the bait with childlike enthusiasm. "Oh, you bet! I'll definitely get that for you." She headed toward a large file cabinet behind her.

"Let's see." She pulled open a drawer and ran her finger over the dozens of files. "Here we go, D, E, F—got it. Sami Firouz." She pulled the file out and placed the folder on her desk, opening it carefully so as not to disrupt the order of the pages. "Dr. Firouz listed two contacts. We reached one."

My heart sank, assuming the family in Knoxville with the Amnesty Organization were the easiest to contact, not the people he might know in Chicago.

"We tried the Johnson's in Knoxville, but they never responded. We reached his cousin in Hyde Park, Chicago."

I could not believe my luck. She wrote the address down on a sticky note. Trying not to appear too rushed now that I possessed what I wanted, I said, "Thank you, Cynthia. Now I've really gotta leave." Not sure why I needed to explain myself, I continued with my lie. "Yes, gotta run. Another conference, you know. And well, you can't keep people waiting for the keynote speaker."

She laughed and then gave me a hug. "God bless you, Mr. Lansing."

I walked down the hall with the sticky note between my thumb and index finger.

Chapter 18

Taking exit 398, I rejoined Interstate 40 traffic and resumed my journey to Chicago. I was on a mission and would not allow this smaller mission of connecting with Dr. Firouz's family to deter me from the original plan. Yes, something drew me to his story and something in me whispered an instruction to close out that chapter of the recent and brief saga. But don't forget, Lansing, that your true purpose, your ultimate goal, remains undeterred. You are still driven by hate.

Perhaps, I rationalized, finding Firouz's family would serve as a convenient cover for what I determined must happen. My anger needed to find its object, and the object needed to suffer. Priscilla's killer needed to suffer. I could not reach Whitlock or Cleon, but this man was within my grasp. If finding Firouz's family helped me reach my goal, then I would use it for my own end.

Hours passed. I vaguely remember taking Highway 640 around Knoxville. I stopped for a milkshake and fuel just after joining I-75 North toward Cincinnati. I then grabbed I-65 North in Indianapolis and began my final leg to Chicago.

The stretch from Indianapolis to Gary, Indiana, was agonizing, but for some reason Sophia loved it. For her, it represented being almost home when we lived in Chicago. The sight and smell of Gary sickened me. Worse yet, the landscape, covered by hundreds of wind turbines, reminded me of a recurring childhood nightmare. In the dream, I tried to escape a monster and found myself running through an open door only to find I had entered the same room with the same monster. That scene would replay in my dreams over and over again. Passing the last wind turbine was like waking up from a nightmare to find myself nearly home.

But where was home now?

When you drive into Chicago, every part of you needs to be alert and prepared for all possibilities. As I moved forward on the Chicago toll road, where it merged with I-94 to become I-90 North, my body, soul, and mind stood on full watch for Chicago's unapologetic style of driving which involved loud horn-blowing, weaving from lane to lane, and the occasional one-middle-finger-wave, as Sophia used to call it, from a driver whom you had accidentally cut off. Taking the exit to East Garfield Boulevard, I began my way toward Hyde Park.

I glanced quickly at my dashboard where I had stuck the address of Dr. Firouz's cousin but knew the more important address, written on an index card, was the address of the man who killed Priscilla. That card, securely placed in my glove compartment, would come out at the appropriate time. I decided to establish some sort of cover, which meant first reaching the Firouz family.

At five in the afternoon, I made the final turn into familiar Washington Park, where Sophia, Priscilla, and I had taken countless walks. Priscilla especially loved throwing breadcrumbs for the ducks that made their home in the lagoon located at the lower end of the park.

I knew Hyde Park like the back of my hand, even after four years. I felt at home making the turn up Woodlawn Avenue, passing the University of Chicago, passing Drexel Square, and slowing down to enjoy the sight of Hyde Park itself with the sound of Chicago's trains rumbling by several hundred yards east. I sighed deeply, trying not to allow the emotions of the moment to blur my purpose. Looking again at the address in my hand, I read it out loud: "Dr. Milad Firouz, 336 Regents Park Apartments." I knew the place well. The fact that Dr. Milad Firouz lived there indicated that he was a man not lacking for money. These luxury apartments were reserved for some of the wealthier inhabitants of Chicago.

Coming into the turn lane of South Hyde Park Boulevard, I noticed the attractive brick siding of the complex and how it maintained its unique identity while compressed against a far narrower apartment complex made of sandstone. The landscaping and well-manicured line of trees made this an attractive place to live as well as an appealing place to drive through. I loved Hyde Park, but remembering the many times the three of us had come here caught me in a wrestling match between who I once was and what I had now become.

I left my car at a nearby parking garage and walked the two blocks to the apartments. A young couple greeted me as I pushed the gate to enter the section marked 300-400. It took just one more minute to find residence 336 but several more minutes to gain my composure and consider how to present myself.

A sudden wave of fatigue swept over me. Why was I doing this? Where would this take me? Gathering my courage, I raised my hand to knock on the door. I noticed my untucked shirt and wondered if my overall appearance looked as disheveled as this portion of my attire. They'll probably think I'm a homeless person, I said to myself. Okay, Andre, stop the foolishness and knock on that dang door.

It took only two knocks before I heard what sounded like the running of a small child. When the footsteps stopped, I envisioned an eager girl or boy standing on the other side of the door remembering instructions to never answer a knock without Mommy or Daddy standing with them. Sure enough, the soft but excited voice of a child yelled, "Daddy, someone's at our door!" The thudding sounds of the heavier footsteps followed.

"Move back, little Pouri," an accented voiced called out, followed by the release of several locks. Then the door cautiously opened, though the protective chain remained in place.

"Excuse me." I moved over about four inches to get a better view of the face peering through the space provided by the taut chain. "Sorry to bother you. I was with your cousin, Sami Firouz, when he died and found myself wanting to know more about him. I happened to be in town and thought I could meet you." I decided to cut to the chase. "My name is

Andre Lansing. I'm the man who rescued him from his car. I am so sorry he died, but I spent a few moments with him just before he…" I was permitted to go no further. The door swung open, and an aggressive arm grabbed me and pulled me into the house.

"Oh my! Oh my! Praise be to Jesus! Come in! Come in! Quick, please come in!" The man was so jubilant that had he been any younger, he would have done cartwheels. My body obeyed the forceful invitation, and once the door shut behind us, I stared into the eyes of three Iranian people gazing at me as if I were a favorite uncle showing up unannounced.

"Mr. Lansing," the man's voice did not lower. "Don't tell me. Oh, praise be to God. Don't tell me. You pulled my cousin, Sami, from the burning car down in Tennessee four months ago? You are that man?"

I nodded to indicate again that, yes, I was that man.

"Unbelievable!" he exclaimed and then grabbed my hand. "My name is Milad. " His grip was hard. "You do not know how many times we talked about you and longed to express our gratitude to you, but we did not know how to contact you."

Hardly able to speak in the face of their enthusiasm, I figured the less I said right now, the better.

"And you say you saw him and talked to him before he died? We did not know that." He walked to a couch and indicated that I should sit in the armchair adjacent. "Oh, how rude of us." He continued, breathless. "You're hungry, aren't you? Jamileh, my dear wife, will get you something."

Jamileh had already gone to the kitchen, so he turned his head in her direction and instructed her to bring some food and hot tea. I was starving. I had not eaten since my stop near Knoxville. But the thought of food didn't capture my attention. Little Pouri did. She appeared to be around six years old. She sat on the floor just two feet from me staring into my eyes. For a moment, she reminded me of Priscilla, which reminded me of the purpose of my trip. As kind as these people were in making me feel welcomed, I refused to allow them or their hospitality to dampen my rage toward the one who had taken my daughter. I was in the presence of good people. There was no doubt of that. But bad people lived out there who did not deserve to live. And one man in particular must answer to me. I was his god. I was his judge.

"Excuse me, Mr. Lansing." Jamileh's soft voice pulled me back to my current surroundings. "Your tea," she offered. "And I cooked some rice and chicken curry if you don't mind that."

We sat together engaging in small talk. I ate. They watched. I answered questions about the trip and how long it took. Finally, Milad noted my fatigue and suggested I spend the night with them. He said we could discuss Sami and the rescue in the morning. I gratefully accepted the offer.

Chapter 19

I slept soundly. The pitter-patter of small footsteps woke me the next morning. I heard the careful voices of parents attempting to keep a six-year-old girl from waking up their guest. I thought again of Priscilla, and I thought again of why I had come here. I turned over to check the time. 6:00 a.m. Not too early to plan my day: find Priscilla's killer, make the final decision about what to do to him, then get away from Chicago. But first, preferably before I left the house, I wanted to discover more about Sami Firouz and the state of his family in Iran.

As I lay in bed, the contrast between the two reasons for coming to Chicago did not escape me. How can one person be set on doing two things so morally polarizing? I came to do right in connecting with Sami's family, and I came to do something harmful to Priscilla's killer. As much as I tried to push aside this tension, I could not. Maybe I put so much weight on knowing more about Sami Firouz because it balanced the wrong I was about to do. Could I justify this? Did I really believe I would leave Chicago feeling I had done the right thing?

I longed for Sophia right now. My heart ached with a deep, inconsolable loss. I badly wanted her advice. Sophia's advice on how to kill a killer? Was I mad? Insane? Had I completely suspended all reason? Where stood the moral framework that had provided the structure of my former life? It had collapsed with Sophia on the living room floor of my house four months ago. Her blood had washed away all previous moral mettle. I had given up on God, and I no longer trusted people. Thus, I lost all restraint. Who was I now?

No one was there to care, to shake a finger at me to say, "Shame on you, Pastor Lansing, for even thinking of such things!" How often I had wanted to blurt out something from the pulpit but did not because I was a reasonable man who allowed the thoughts but never the expression of those thoughts. What was the difference, though, between thinking things and acting on them? The two now merged, and I celebrated it. I was one man instead of two conflicted men. This was my base nature moving by impulse to do what was just, and as I stared again at the fan blades moving slowly in the room in Chicago, I was settled. I was justified.

My name is Anger, and I'm quite okay with that. Before, I covered my true nature and its impulses, instead doing what others concluded to be right. What would Sophia say? I am sure I could have convinced her of my profound discovery. The discovery that I never really owned my convictions but functioned for years off the convictions of others. I assumed a faith because I saw it work in others. When it stopped working in my life, I gave up on it. All this happened in the past four months.

I could easily rationalize this way of thinking because I was removed from the constraints of church. People no longer needed me to behave a certain way. Leading a life prescribed by a consensus of people no longer defined me. As I continued to stare at the spinning blades of the ceiling fan, I wondered how many other pastors were as duped as I was—their true feelings, their true impulses shoved down by hierarchical expectations imposed on them but not really their own. They were the ones in conflict.

"What I do not want to do, I find myself doing," the apostle Paul wrote. "And when I want to do what is right, evil is right there with me." Paul called this the law of death. If he had given in to his impulses, he would not have been torn between his two natures. Paul could have been free. His struggle would not have been so intense. He could have spared himself a great deal of anguish if he had just given in to what truly lay in his heart.

Now that I had given up on church, I felt comfortable with the idea of functioning without God. I was not living in conflict as I had before. This scared me a little. I knew what I was capable of. I knew what I was planning to do. The only restraint now was knowing where my actions might land me. I was not held back by moral principles but by the impractical outcome of my proposed action. My present conflict was no longer with right or wrong. Instead, I wondered if I could really get away with it.

A soft knock interrupted my thoughts. Jamileh asked if I wanted coffee or something to eat. I quickly put on shorts, shrugged on my shirt, and opened the door. Jamileh was a very attractive woman, perhaps in her early forties. Her olive skin reminded me of Sophia's following a sun-soaked vacation near the ocean. Jamileh, like Sophia, had gentle eyes and hair that settled softly on her shoulders. The sight of her standing at the door saddened me. Yet I could do nothing to reclaim my loss, so I told her that a cup of coffee is the best way to start my day.

Several minutes later, I joined Milad and Jamileh at the table. The smell of coffee and the sight of scrambled eggs and bacon made Milad's invitation to breakfast impossible to turn down. Milad offered a prayer of thanks for the food and for the day and for all God's blessings, and as they began to eat, I came fully awake with the aid of the coffee. Several moments passed in silence. Milad unsuccessfully tried to hold back a belch before he grabbed his napkin, wiped the corners of his mouth, then folded the napkin again and placed it under his fork.

"Tell me, Mr. Lansing, where exactly are you from? What do you do? And how did you happen upon my cousin on that fatal day?" Milad looked at me before quickly adding, "Oh, and Mr. Lansing? This is Saturday. We do not work today, so we have all the time in the world. Perhaps you need to do some things though, so just let us know when you need to leave."

Jamileh cleared her throat as though to remind him of something.

"Oh, yes. One more thing. We don't know how long you're planning to stay, but we hope you will come to church with us tomorrow. It is not far from here. Many Iranians attend, but the service is in English, and I think you would be greatly blessed by it. Besides, I'm eager for you to meet our pastor. I think you might find him interesting. Okay now, I've gone long enough. Please," he chuckled, tapping his finger down. "The table is now yours. Literally!"

I paused for a moment, wondering how much I should share about myself. Then I realized that the more I said, the easier this would be for me. I saw no reason to make things up but also no reason to tell him everything that had transpired. He certainly did not need to know about the accusations of rape, but why not share about Sophia's death and, if necessary, Priscilla's passing? So I told both Milad and Jamileh almost everything. I was a pastor in a small town in Tennessee. Before this, I worked in Chicago. Four years into my ministry in Tennessee, I was accused of something that was devastating to me and to Sophia. I wanted to run, and I did run, and I met Sami because of it. Following a night in a hotel and the brief time with Sami the next day and his sudden death, I returned home to face the accusations.

One day later, I met with a trusted friend and also made an unsuccessful appeal to a police officer I had called my friend. He warned me that a man who carried a vendetta had threatened me and my wife. I rushed home. When I arrived, that man held my wife while his nephew aimed his rifle at her head. A confrontation ensued. My wife was shot. Both men were arrested and awaiting trial, but it could be months before a venue was set and a jury selected. I had resigned from my church, and now my life was empty.

Often when we had visited with people, Sophia kicked me under the table when I crossed a line and said too much. I did not need help to be uninhibited. It came naturally to me. I talked easily, and according to Sophia, I trusted people too much. One of my problems, she often said, was assuming that people understood my words, assuming everyone liked me and saw my heart. But Sophia knew better. Time, particularly time in Lowensville, proved her right. She would often say, "Andre, assume everyone you talk to gossips. Just assume it. You will find yourself a lot more cautious in conversations." This was one among many things Sophia had said that I now wished I had paid more attention to. Of course, she was nearly always right.

I did not share with Milad or Jamileh about losing Priscilla, suddenly fearing that doing so betrayed my mission. Seeing I had no more to share, Milad pushed his chair back, stood, and suggested we adjourn to the living room to continue the conversation. I complied. We moved to the larger room. Milad waved me to a chair, then looked intently at me. "You're on more than one journey, aren't you, Andre?"

This propensity to pry, but also to be accurate, was a trait Milad obviously shared with his cousin, Sami. I remembered how Sami so quickly commented on my fear and how I tried unsuccessfully to deflect it. Afraid that Milad wanted to pursue a similar path of inquiry, I quickly changed the subject. Ignoring his comment about being on more than one journey, I suggested this would be an excellent time to know more about Sami. After all, it was why I had come.

"When I met Sami, he told me he was on his way here, to Chicago, to meet someone with information about his wife and child back in Iran." This seemed to raise Milad's interest considerably. Noticing his anxious expression, I continued. "From what he told me, he fled Iran to protect his family, but if I recall correctly, he had not heard from them in over ten years. Do you know more about this? After all, it's one of the reasons—I mean, it's the reason I came to Chicago."

Milad did not seem to notice my near slip of revealing multiple reasons for coming to Chicago. If he did catch it, he did not let on. He did seem eager to talk.

"Oh my. You talk about a dramatic story and a dramatic life! So tragic that with all the good coming for Sami and his family, he is not here to see it. We believe God in His Sovereignty orchestrated this. For His own reasons, He needed Sami out of the story in order to finish His story. I find that God often works that way. We like for Him to be neat and ordered in all He does, but I'm discovering more and more that this is not how He works."

I wanted to blurt out, "You're not telling me anything I don't know, brother," but kept the comment to myself.

"Mr. Lansing, or should I call you Pastor Lansing?"

"Mr. Lansing will do." Right now, I preferred it.

Smiling, he continued. "Mr. Lansing, let me tell you first a little about myself, because it will help make better sense of Sami's story. Do you have time?"

“All the time in the world,” I said.

I took note that Milad wrung his hands as he spoke. When he paused for my response, his hands opened toward me as though to invite a response. I found it engaging.

“Sami and I were very close back in Iran, but when we finished high school, he went on to study medicine, and I went on to study nuclear physics. You heard, I'm sure, about Iran and all the concerns about nuclear research.”

The hands stopped wringing. I nodded to indicate that, yes, I was familiar with it. In the news for months, the situation had many in the USA worried.

His hands resumed wringing. “Slated with hundreds of other students to serve in the foundation of Iran’s research program, I went to college in Germany, but Sami, strangely enough, traveled to Switzerland to study medicine. We saw each other several times a year, but during the third year in his course of studies, he changed. We were both devout Muslims. When I visited him or when he called, we discussed our studies. But that year Sami wanted to talk about Christianity.”

Milad paused and took a sip from a cup placed earlier by Jamileh on the coffee table between us. He wiped his mouth with his right palm and continued. Hands wringing. “It scared me. I warned him often that he should not talk about such things. Yet, curious, I allowed him to share enough to feel safe about it. One time while visiting each other, he brought a friend with him. The man, a devout Christian, had turned Sami toward Christianity. What I heard from this man about

Jesus captivated me, but what baffled me the most was Sami's joy over discovering Christ. I will not bore you with the details, but suffice it to say, I joined my cousin as a follower of Jesus."

I think Milad expected me to show elation over this piece of information. I forced a smile. "Wow. Fantastic. Especially in that part of the world."

"Yes, indeed. Very unusual." The hands kept wringing. "It was very hard for me to pursue nuclear science, but I managed to work in the industry for ten years before escaping with my wife. Sami? Not so fortunate. He became a doctor, but unlike me, he spoke bravely about his faith."

Milad lowered his head, and his voice grew somber. "I just ran. He stayed and talked openly about his faith."

I sensed Milad was revisiting some old feelings of guilt as he spoke. Finally gathering himself, he continued. "Sami married a beautiful daughter of the Iranian ambassador to Switzerland, whom he met while in school, but his outspokenness after several years placed such pressure on him and his wife, Mehrnoosh, that Sami realized he needed to leave for the sake of his family. Only Iranians understand this, but the way government officials communicate threats is frightening. It dawned on Sami one day that the only way to protect his wife and young boy was to flee. Taking the whole family was not as easy for him as it was for me.

"One day, while attending a medical conference in Germany, Sami escaped. He met officials with an amnesty group. Of course you know of the family in Tennessee who took him in for these past years."

All this was interesting, but it wasn't quite what I wanted to know. "So what did he hear recently that led him to believe he could reunite with his family?"

"Ah, that part is fascinating," Milad explained. "Five months ago, I heard through some of my contacts in Iran that Sami's father-in-law, the ambassador to Switzerland, faced serious trouble with the government. I'm not sure of the details, but it involved an accusation against him for stealing money. I believe he felt this was due to Mehrnoosh's marriage to Sami. It was the government's way of punishing Sami's family. The ambassador was able to escape with Mehrnoosh and her son just in time. When I contacted Sami about this, they were in Germany, making their way to the United States. That is when you met Sami. He was on his way here when the accident happened."

My heart sank. It added to my frustration over the way God seemed to do things. The way God seemed to work disturbed me. I was tired of the clichés thrown around by Christians following Priscilla's death. They seemed so shallow.

After our daughter's death, I cringed when Christians said things like, "I will pray for you," or, "You are in my prayers." "Really?" I wanted to call out. "Do you mean that, or is that just a way to deflect the matter to God?" It seemed for most people, when faced with a friend's burden they were perfectly capable of helping carry, it became far easier to pass the matter to God. You're off the hook, right? Is that it? Oh, and by the way, how did it turn out for you? Did the prayer work? Were such people satisfied that they had done their part by promising to pray? Did they follow up to see if God answered their prayer? Or was that never the point? How often people say they are His hands, His voice, and His feet, but in the fairytale world of "Isn't life good in God's kingdom?" people find their way around saying things that they don't really mean.

In my growing cynicism, I often pictured Moses after meeting God at the burning bush. I envisioned him leaving that place, still trembling, and running into a fellow shepherd who just lost his mother-in-law. What would this Moses, who had just encountered the frightening and yet embracing holiness of God, say to this grieving workmate? "Hey, buddy. God is good all the time, man. Just trust Him. He'll comfort you. And, oh yeah, you'd better believe it, bro—I'll pray for you."

Shouldn't our view of God shape our responses to each other?

Things like this—Sami's death coinciding with the great news of his wife and son's rescue—explained why I stopped saying what I really did not mean. I stopped expecting God to make sense. Priscilla's death did not make me a spiritual cynic but a harsh realist. Until Sophia's death, this realism was an asset. It made me deeply sensitive to the way I spoke to people. I rarely offered my prayers to others but only because I now took prayer seriously. After her death, I stopped caring.

Sophia had been proud of my no-nonsense faith following Priscilla's death. But Sophia was not here to keep me focused, was she? I tired of this tension where God, on one hand, rescued His children out of Iran but offered another on the sacrificial altar of a Tennessee interstate.

Milad observed my silence by placing his hand on my knee and patting it a few times. "Isn't it marvelous how God works?"

"What did you just say?" His disjointed comment took me aback. He seemed to sense my unease and graciously turned the question into an observation.

"It is marvelous to me how God works. Yet you struggle with that, don't you? Probably because it doesn't fit into your neatly prescribed sense of God. Am I right?"

I shifted in my chair, growing uncomfortable with this conversation. Milad did not seem to notice, his voice growing in excitement. "Mr. Lansing, Sami's wife, his son, and her father are in Chicago. We plan to see them this week. I would love for you to meet them, but I want you to meet someone else first, someone you need to talk to."

I said this would be fine but informed him that I would be spending this afternoon on several errands. I told him I would very much like to take him up on his offer to stay with his family. But this family's appeal would not distract me from what I had determined to do in the next few hours.

Chapter 20

I excused myself from the living room with the explanation that I needed to leave for my errands within the hour. I needed to shower and then look over some details on a map I brought with me. If curious about my plans, they did not show it. I thanked Jamileh for a wonderful breakfast, shook hands with Milad, and thanked him for the information about Sami, then retreated to my room.

An hour later, Milad waved good-bye as I closed the door behind me. Ten minutes later, I was in my car. Leaning over, I opened the glove compartment; my shaking hands betrayed both the nervousness and, strangely, the excitement of seeing the address of the man who took my daughter's life. Tucked in a protective casing behind the index card was the Smith & Wesson .38 Special revolver I had bought before starting this journey.

After checking that both the index card and the revolver remained in place, I sat in my car for a few moments, considering my next move. I wondered first how long I should stay. Leaving town too quickly might attract the attention of anyone who had met me. Staying for a day or two might make me look less suspicious. I could carry out my plan, spend one more night with Milad, attend church, and leave Sunday afternoon without attracting much attention.

Then I rehearsed the history of the gun which I purchased at a local pawn shop in Lowensville. Both the gun and bullets were untraceable. Without my asking, the man who sold me the gun informed me that no paperwork was necessary, including no background check, and if I gave him $450 he would ask no questions at all. Furthermore, he assured me he possessed such a bad memory and would not recognize me if he saw me downtown an hour later.

I repeated the address out loud and punched the details into my GPS. The male voice on my TomTom told me that the home on East 108 and South Fox Avenue was exactly 8.2 miles away with an estimated time, barring any traffic, of twenty-four minutes. I threw my car into reverse, thankful that I had not brought my pickup truck. It alone would have made me stand out, particularly in the more sophisticated parts of Chicago.

It took half an hour to drive to South Deering, the part of Chicago where the man lived. It was a rougher part of the city, and I knew it well from my days working at the food bank. After a left on South Colfax and a quick right on South Bensley, the TomTom warned me that I was only minutes from my destination. As I took the final turn, about to do something that could land me in prison, I found myself uttering a prayer. Out of habit—mere habit!—I found myself unconsciously committing my act to God. It was bizarre.

Fortunately, I stopped myself before I could actually make the request.

The man who killed my daughter lived on this street. In my car was the gun that would take his life. In my heart and in my mind lay the determination to go through with it. The clarity of mind surprised me. So this is what it is like to murder someone, I thought to myself.

The voice on the TomTom announced that the house stood to my left. The address in Sophia's journal now matched perfectly with the house thirty yards from where I pulled my car to a stop. 63 South Fox Avenue.

Taking a deep breath, I moved my hand toward the glove compartment. The snap of the compartment latch seemed unusually loud as did the sound of my hand rustling past the owner's manual and other essential papers to reach into the case that held the gun. I pulled out the case, set it on the passenger seat, closed the glove box, and took a deep breath. That, too, seemed unusually loud.

"Well, here we go," I finally said to myself. My hands opened the case gingerly as if it held a sensitive high explosive. I carefully lifted the gun. As the sun glistened over the smooth barrel of the revolver, I removed one bullet wrapped in a cloth and hidden in an indented area inside of the case. Using the cloth to make sure I left no fingerprints on the bullet, I placed the bullet in the open cylinder and closed it with pressure from my left palm. I was ready to do what I had come to do.

Chapter 21

South Fox Avenue seemed unusually empty for a Saturday afternoon, but the mid-July day offered a blistering reason for folks to stay indoors. As I stepped out of the car, I could hear the drone of air conditioners echoing in a symphonic rhythm, adding an eerie background sound as I walked toward the house. The walk from my car to the killer's house seemed to take more time than it actually did but not because I had second thoughts. I had never been so determined to do something. I did not care what anyone thought of me. No one paid attention to my life right now anyway. I was, in the truest sense of the word, a loner. Loners move alone. Loners do not care what others say about them. A loner can move stealthily toward his mission because the obsession with that mission makes him a loner.

Just a few feet from the steps of house number 63, I went through my mental checklist. Check the gun. Both hands out of pockets. Stand confidently but not aggressively near the door. Turn shoulder slightly to a slant and knock. Positioned, I raised my right hand and knocked carefully. The casual knock of a mailman or of a neighbor coming over to borrow some sugar or, on a day like this, some ice.

I heard footsteps. Each step seem to match the beating in my chest. Stay calm, Andre. Stay focused. Stay on mission. Similar to when I had first knocked on Milad's door, several latches released from the inside. There was no peephole in the door. This was highly to my advantage. The door creaked open. To my disappointment, I faced the sad, dark eyes of an elderly woman.

"Yes, can I help you?" came a soft, shaky voice. She kept her mouth hidden behind the door, allowing only her eyes to peer through the opening.

"I hope so," I stammered. With all the planning, I had not prepared to speak to someone else. I assumed the person who answered the door would be Priscilla's killer. After the accident, Sophia had told me that the man was white and in his mid-thirties. Before me stood an elderly woman. The mother or grandmother of the killer?

"I…I…was just wondering…I mean, is there a young man… uh, a man in his thirties or so living here?"

"What's this about?" The sad eyes said, speaking for the mouth I could not see.

I needed to come up with something quickly. "Well, Ma'am, I met him last week at a bar, and we, um, we talked a lot and became friends. He never told me his name. He, um, did give me his address, and…"

"Are you asking about Bronson?" Her voice shook with anger. I worried that the woman would close the door. "Is this a joke? Bronson didn't meet you last week. He died three years ago."

I felt a rush of anger along with a sudden sense of defeat. My shoulders grew limp, and my face, I know, burned beet-red. Her eyes lifted as she took in my sudden change of demeanor. Surprisingly, she unbolted the door and opened it wide. Though she did not invite me in, she did come out.

After closing the door, she hobbled over to a rocking chair tucked snugly into the small space on the front porch. I stepped back to make way for her as she attempted to sit without falling in the process.

The two of us said nothing for a few moments. The chair rocked as I stared out into the street. She finally broke the silence. "My Bronson. My only child. He was a good boy. A very good boy. Attended university here in Chicago, got his degree in business. After he graduated, he worked at National Trust Bank just a few blocks from here. Five years ago, his world collapsed."

At her reference to five years ago, I turned my head and looked at her intently.

"He couldn't live with himself after what happened."

"What did happen?" I asked.

"It was too much for Bronson. After the accident—and it was an accident—yes, he drank but that was never the cause. You see, Mister, he took someone's life. He lost control of his car. It veered off the road and hit a small girl riding a bicycle. After six months in jail, he lost his job, lost his fiancée. He couldn't take it anymore. Three years ago, he killed himself."

If Bronson's mother had looked at me, she would have seen a man drained of all color. The collision of two tragedies jolted me. Maddening rage again filled me. A rush of hate and the realization that I had lost the object of my anger weakened me. For the past several weeks, I had focused that rage on one man. I had lived preparing for this. My rage sought its resting place. Anger would be satisfied knowing that one wrong had been righted. Justice would be carried out. Dr. Sommeral had been right. Anger needed an object. I had found one and given it a name, the only name I knew—Priscilla's killer.

But to the woman sitting next to me, who continued to rock while lost in her own thoughts, the name was more personal. Bronson. A strange irony. Two strangers, yards apart from each other, both lived in the vacuum of the loss of the same person. Bronson's death robbed her of love; Bronson's death stole my purpose. We were both unsure, both alone.

She looked up at me. "Why are you really here? You didn't meet Bronson last week. We both know that." She seemed to have little energy left when she asked this, as though my presence drained her of her last reserve.

In my utter selfishness, I possessed neither the interest nor the strength to answer her question. The man I knew a year ago as Andre Lansing was not the man who callously walked away from that woman having failed in his mission and unsure which way to go next. As had happened four months ago, a frightening numbness began to settle over me as I walked back toward my car. If I had been the old Andre, I would have felt the curious and stinging stare of a broken woman utterly confused over this strange meeting with a man who seemed to appear from nowhere.

I did not notice. I did not care.

Chapter 22

There are two choices every human makes when confronted with a tragedy: give up or keep going. Sophia loved to tell the story of a time when she was eleven years old. Following an hour or two of touch football with boys and girls on her street, her father interrupted and urged her to come back home for dinner. Obedient and hungry, Sophia found no reason to argue, and since the ball they played with was hers, she excused herself, took the ball, and began to walk home. She had not taken three steps when a boy who lived just two doors down from her, Johnny Rolaski, yelled out, "You're just a quitter." Sophia stopped, turned slowly, dropped the ball, and proceeded to beat Johnny up. If Sophia's dad had not pulled her away, no doubt Johnny would have sustained some serious injuries.

Sophia had never been a quitter and because of it, neither was I. However, I considered quitting now. I had nowhere to go and no idea what to do. So I got back into my car and just drove. I lost all focus and kept driving. Two hours passed. In a moment of lucidity, I noticed I was no longer in my car but sitting on a bench in Millennium Park in downtown Chicago.

Somehow I had managed to park and walk two blocks, even cross several streets, all in an aimless state of detachment. Crowds moved purposefully around me, but I had not noticed them. Just thirty yards in front of me stood the imposing site of The Bean. The mirrored ball was a popular destination with tourists and Priscilla's favorite place to visit on our many trips here.

I could still picture Priscilla running through the narrow gap at the shallow base of The Bean, giggling as she glimpsed a gigantic and distorted version of herself reflected off the surface of the ball. Sitting on the bench just yards away, with my own need for reflection, I felt my former self as if emerging from the dead, intent on battling the broken man I had become. I joined Paul in his cry of, "Who will rescue me from this body of death?" Unlike Paul, I did not have the answer.

A familiar voice woke me to my surroundings. Standing next to me, looking down into my dazed, weary eyes, were Milad and his little girl, Pouri.

"Mr. Lansing, oh my goodness! Mr. Lansing. In a city this size, what are the chances of meeting you like this? Pouri and I decided to come down here, and when she looked into the mirrored bean, she saw you and kept yelling, 'Look, Papa! Look, it's Mr. Lansing. On the bench!' She pointed at your reflection. And here you are. She was right. It is Mr. Lansing." He laughed but suddenly stopped. "Mr. Lansing," Milad turned somber. "You look like—you Americans say: Like you have been run over by a bulldozer."

It's a truck, I wanted to say.

"Are you all right?" he continued. "Did something happen to you? You look very dejected."

Since pushing away Dr. Sommeral, I had not wanted anyone to care for me, but Milad's words worked like jackhammer blows bent on weakening a well-fortified dam. I felt the concrete I used to create that wall begin to crumble. I pushed back to maintain my barrier but could not. My body began to throb. My shoulders shook. There on that bench, as the world kept moving around me, the dam burst, and a flood of emotions poured out, a release of anguish and hate.

Milad sat beside me, but I did not look up. My head bent low in a futile attempt to hide my tears. He said nothing. After a few moments, his arm moved across my back, and his hand squeezed my shoulder. Still, he remained quiet. We sat this way, my dam disintegrated by battering emotions thrown against it.

I had often been in his position, attempting to console but not knowing what to say. Sometimes I said more than needed and stupid things at that. But Milad sat silent as the wall inside me crumbled. When the last shard fell, there poured out a final emptying. When no more tears existed, I raised my hands and wiped my eyes. I had no tissue, so I used my shirt. Then I remembered the time Sophia and I broke up for a season back in college.

She met me one day outside her college dormitory where we often met to walk to breakfast. I noticed she was not herself. She wasted no time explaining why.

"Andre," I remembered her saying, "I don't think we can keep dating. I don't feel confident that God is calling me into the ministry. I need some time to fast and pray about this."

So we broke up. I tried to move on with my life, but I was miserable alone. Two weeks later, while seated on a wall where students often relaxed in the center of campus, I noticed Sophia walking toward me for the first time since our break up. She had done a good job of secluding herself from me and an even better job of ignoring the multiple phone calls I made to her dorm floor. She suggested we walk to the pond at the edge of the campus and talk. My heart raced, and my hopes rose. Surely we would get back together again.

We found a log on the little sandy beach and sat down. We both commented at the same time how our relationship started here. Usually, she showed me the scar on her foot and laughing said, "See what you did to me, buddy? Are you sorry yet?" I would respond with, "Of course I'm not sorry! Best catch I ever made." This time, we bypassed our nostalgia.

"So, Soph, what's up?"

Excited, she began to tell me all God had taught her during her sabbatical from our relationship. She went on and on about God's love for her and how she was adopted by Him as His child—as special to God as Jesus was to Him. As I waited for her to relate this to our relationship, she suddenly began to cry. When Sophia cried, especially in a sudden switch from being jubilant about something, I knew I was in for an outpouring of emotions. Between sobs, she explained that she missed me so much and could not imagine living without me. She told me she had not intended to get back with me but had just wanted to talk and share what God taught her. Sitting there, something gave way, and she realized she needed me.

Tears streamed from her eyes. Snot gushed from her nose. Instinctively, I took off my shirt, wiped her nose, and urged her to blow. I put that shirt back on and wore it the rest of the day. "True love is messy," she always said when referring back to that moment.

Milad broke the long silence. "Mr. Lansing, I cannot claim to understand what you are going through. Not at all. After you left this morning, Jamileh and I got on our knees and prayed for you because we saw you caught in a dark tunnel of some kind. We could not, or should not, say anything except that God was not complete with whatever he asked you to undergo. But Mr. Lansing, I believe you're now at the end of something horrible, and here, rock bottom, you're ready to look up and see something you never knew existed."

His words filled me with something I had not had for years. Hope. Yet, I could only look at him, afraid that if I spoke there would be more tears.

"Mr. Lansing, I can say nothing more. Come, my friend. Come with me back to my house. It's time to freshen up, eat something, and rest. I want you to meet someone tomorrow.

I believe you are ready to meet him." He moved his eyes away from mine. "Yes, I believe you are ready now to meet this person."

Soon I was in his home, lying on the guest bed. Too tired to even eat, I fell into a very deep sleep.

Chapter 23

A streak of sunlight pushed through the blinds. The stunning array of rainbow colors refracted by the light blue glass vase on the dresser near the bed woke me. I stared at it, wondering if I would have noticed something like this a day or even a month before. Ten minutes passed and the stream of light, creating this show for me in the room, moved slightly away from the vase. As it did, the colors faded. Intrigued, I kept my eyes fastened on the light until the colors disappeared.

On the end of the bed lay a towel and washcloth. I forced myself up and moved slowly across the room to open the blinds which allowed more light inside. Again, would I have cared a day or even a month ago?

Sophia often teased me about my need for natural light. The moment I walked into a room curtains had to be opened. I attributed it to growing up in the tropics, where the sun always shone brightly. Something in me was different this morning. Certainly tired, I did not regret the way the previous day turned out. Still depressed, yes. But I was surprised to realize I was not numb. The fact that I cared about the amount of light in the room, that I paid attention to the dark red color of the towel and washcloth, told me something had changed. There was also no impulse to push away these feelings as there was yesterday.

A quick glance at the clock told me I had about an hour and fifteen minutes before Milad said we would head for church. I spent forty-five of those minutes in the shower. The water felt good. I allowed myself to enjoy every drop that flowed from the shower-head to massage my body. As the water hit the back of my neck, calmness filled me. I chuckled at myself standing in this shower without feeling rushed. I had no plans. No ideas racing through my head. Everything was still. Right now, for this moment, everything seemed good.

An hour later, I found myself sitting next to Pouri in the backseat of the sleek green Saab. The church, Milad explained, met in a storefront just five miles away. This would be my first visit to a church in over four months. It had been years since I attended church as a congregant rather than a preacher. Even in my previous life here in Chicago, rarely did a Sunday go by when I was not preaching somewhere.

In ten minutes, we pulled into a gravel parking lot. Milad parked in one of the few spaces left in the back of a building, near a weathered door marked "Personnel Only." Pouri grabbed my hand as we strolled ahead of Milad and Jamileh. I smiled, feeling an inner warmth I had not felt in years. The small hand holding mine did not bring any painful memories of Priscilla as it had yesterday. Rather, the memories caressed and renewed my beat-up soul. I walked the thirty yards to the front of the building with curious anticipation. Pouri held my hand, but another hand also pulled me toward this place and this moment, a hand I believed had callously let go of me long ago. I wondered now if I had been wrong.

A tall man greeted Pouri and me at the door. His broad smile made her giggle. She sure loves life, I thought to myself. He turned to me and reached out his hand. "I'm Charlie. Milad called and told me he had a guest staying. I just want to say that we love you, and we thank Jesus for you."

This struck me as odd but made me feel good and welcome in this unimpressive place of worship. I felt embarrassed as I remembered the greeting classes back in Lowensville where I lectured on the importance of body language and saying the right things, particularly to church guests.

"Did we ever talk about sincerity?" I wondered as Charlie yelled over my shoulder, still holding my hand, to welcome Milad and Jamileh. What I did back home seemed so stiff by comparison—an orchestration of perception that spoke more about impressions than authentic love. This man had not rehearsed his greeting as I instructed folks back home to do. "Practice at home with your husband," I lectured, "and work on your body language and smile. Yes, of course, Martha, stand in front of your mirror and look at yourself, see yourself as others see you while you greet them Sunday morning. Practice makes perfect, and we want to welcome people with perfection."

Still holding my hand, Pouri yanked me toward the aisle. "Mr. Lansing, we sit here. I can see the man with the guitar best from right here, unless of course, that fat woman—although

Mummy tells me not to call her that—sits right in front of me. Her name is Mrs. Simmons, and I think she sits there on purpose, but Daddy just moves me over. I asked him why he doesn't move the fat woman over instead of always me. But we must love Mrs. Simmons, so we do. Mummy says if we keep loving someone, we will end up wanting to love them." Here she covered her mouth with her free hand. "Daddy says, 'Yes, there is much to love in Mrs. Simmons.'"

We sat down in a row of chairs with several empty spaces. The room looked full but only because it was a small room. The walls, made out of brick, looked as though the building had been turned inside out. Only sixty feet by ninety feet, there were about fifty people in the room. I bet they don't care about attendance, I smiled to myself.

A man with a blond ponytail stood in the front, playing a guitar, and bopping his head slightly to the beat. He wore jeans and a T-shirt. The people in the room, as though on cue —but I think it was spontaneous—joined him in the familiar chorus. I did not see many people in conversation with each other but only because it seemed they gathered to worship God, not to fellowship. Yet a love for one another seemed to flow from that reverence. I felt it. Back home, this would have bothered me. But here it seemed right. In Lowensville, we encouraged people to talk freely before the service as the music played in the background, but here I sensed the fellowship was first with God, and people were comfortable with that.

Milad and Jamileh joined Pouri and me just as the man on the guitar completed his song. For several minutes, there was silence. Far from awkward, the silence offered its own call to worship, an unspoken invitation to prepare one's heart and receive cleansing to meet God. The man with the ponytail leafed through several pages of music, settled on a song, and began to play softly again. Without instruction, people stood up and sang. We reflected first on the holiness of God. Several shouted as we mused over God's love for us. The final two songs spoke again of His majesty and holiness, and there were more shouts of praise. I looked around and noticed some raised hands, but what caught my attention was the number of people who wept as we sang. The heartfelt response to God expressed in music tugged on emotional strings but in a way that did not seem sentimental, just honest. Emotions tracking with the mind as a response to truth. I had never worshipped so simply and so beautifully as I did in that plain house of worship.

When the singing concluded, Charlie, the greeter, asked us to stand again for the reading of the scripture. The words by the Apostle Paul about the humility of Jesus and His call for us to possess His attitude awakened me to a reality lost in my life for far too long—that others existed around me. As he read further of Jesus' obedience even to death, I quickly reflected on my own history of loving others. I loved others in order to be loved in return. My love was not a selfless love but one that I offered with the hope of being appreciated. I had often read this scripture, but I never really heard the message. This day, something drew me to the love of Jesus in a way that awakened a new desire, a desire to be loved so I could love. This was a love foreign to me, and I longed for it.

Charlie closed his Bible and asked God to bless the reading of the Word for today. Again, silence. And for the first time since arriving, I wondered who the preacher was. No one fitting that description caught my attention when we walked in. I saw no one dressed to impress others. There was no one wearing an air of importance and commanding the center of attention that once mattered to me.

In the past, I needed to make myself known as the pastor. I positioned myself to be seen. I spoke to be heard. I said things to impress. I hugged and patted backs to be appreciated. No one in this small room fit that description. I had no idea who pastored this church until the man with the ponytail, dragging the music stand with him, placed himself and the stand on the stage and asked us to look again at the passage Charlie read from.

"That's our pastor," Pouri piped up loud enough to get a few chuckles from those in the row behind us. "He's really cool, and his name is Carson." Milad patted her knee to instruct her to be quiet but not until she added, "I like pulling his ponytail, and I think he likes it, too." More chuckling sounded behind us.

Carson, the pastor, spoke with a soft but clear voice. Following his reading, he explained that his topic today was "Jesus, Comfortable in His Own Skin." Odd title, I thought to myself, but intriguing just the same. According to the apostle Paul in the passage we just read, Jesus came to earth fully God but also fully human. He lived in bodily form with all the same human characteristics and vulnerabilities as we do. He lived in His human body while still fully God. During

His life on earth, Jesus depended on His Father as a human does but was never less God in doing so. He chose to suspend His ability to draw from His godhood when faced with temptation and troubles. He encountered life as human and as God.

Carson gave a brief history lesson on the church's understanding of the two natures of Jesus. It was not until AD 451, at the Council of Chalcedon, that a definite statement about Jesus' two natures was written. This was necessary because all sorts of heresies threatened the integrity of the church. One school of thought, led by a guy named Athanasius, stressed Jesus' divinity more than His humanity. The other end of the rope was held by those who were influenced by the Greek philosopher, Aristotle, and who saw Jesus as a unity of body, soul, and spirit. This led to a belief that saw equality but distinction in both natures of Jesus.

"Many confuse the two natures of Jesus," Carson continued, "for two different personalities. Many assume that part of Jesus was human and the other part divine. But this is not accurate. We should not see Jesus as having two personalities but as having one—one both completely human and completely God. Theologians call this the 'hypostatic union,'" Carson informed us. "When Jesus was born as human, His divinity became one with His humanity. They were one substance. He did not live in conflict between two natures, struggling between the spiritual and the physical. He lived comfortably in His own skin."

As Carson spoke, I found myself overwhelmed by these thoughts. Perhaps I knew this distinction, and very possibly I preached about the same thing, but I don't believe I had ever fully considered it. Yes, I believed that Jesus was both divine and human during His life on earth, but this was a theological concept to me, never a motivation for trust. Was it possible, I thought, still focused on every word from Carson, that Jesus' ease in living for God as human means we, too, can be comfortable in our own skin?

Carson seemed to read my mind. His voice increased in passion as he drew his message to a close. "Jesus wasn't unique from us," Carson stressed. "We assume Jesus had it easier because He was also God. I mean, come on, God can handle any problem, right? After all, He is God, right?"

Some people chuckled at Carson's questions. He moved away from the center of the stage and stepped into the aisle separating the two sides of the room.

I bowed my head and stared at the floor, considering his application, suddenly faced with a renewed appreciation for the incarnation of Jesus and the implications of that for us. No, it was not easier for Jesus. In some sense, it was harder for Him because He had His godhood that He could manipulate to His own advantage. He chose to suffer; I had not. He willingly faced the cross; I did not. Priscilla's and Sophia's deaths were forced on me. Had I been given a choice in their deaths, I would not have accepted those paths. Jesus had an out but chose the cross over the out.

The truth wrapped itself around my weakened body and clothed me with a renewed hope that this was not the end for me. I felt invigorated spiritually and enabled to view what I could never see before. What Jesus suffered was meant for moments like mine. I knew it. I had taught it. But I never embraced it.

It was now embracing me.

When I raised my head, I saw that Carson had bowed his, holding his guitar, seated on the stool again. He thanked God for His Word and the Holy Spirit for His presence and Jesus for His simple example of living His human life in complete obedience to His Father. He praised God that we, too, do not need to live in conflict between two natures but can also be comfortable in our skin as adopted children of God, that the presence of God living in us can live in harmony with our own nature and consume us to the point where our body of flesh contains only one nature. Then he thanked God that our battle between the spiritual and the flesh can end when we allow Jesus to bring us to the end of ourselves.

His last statement rocked my world. Our battle between the spiritual and the flesh can end, and will end, when we—when I—allow Jesus to bring me to the end of myself. The words made sense because I could go no lower. I was dying. I was dead. No hand had reached out to rescue me because God could not redeem me until I reached the end.

Oh, God. I understand now. You allowed Priscilla to die. You took Sophia from me. You permitted the accusations. And in your mystery and sovereignty, You used all these as certain and final blows to cause my death.

No, I did not believe God passively stood by as these tragedies hit my life, hoping they would bring me to my end. He was not a passive but an active participant. He initiated them.

Carson led the congregation in a final, jubilant song about the cross and the One who bled on that cross to forgive us of sin. Voices shouted in unison that Jesus was forsaken for their acceptance and how, because He was condemned, they were now alive and well. On that final note, Carson struck his fingers strong against the guitar strings as amens and applause filled the room. There was no closing prayer, no benediction. Carson placed his guitar on the front row of chairs, fell to his knees at one of the few empty chairs, and bowed his head in his hands as his elbows rested on the seat. Around me, others sat down. Some joined Carson in kneeling at their seats. It was again quiet. Ten minutes passed until, one by one, people began to stand, a few speaking to one another, others comfortably walking out of the place of worship.

Pouri, seated to my left, crawled over my knee and made a hasty run to several girls her age sitting on the steps of the stage. I felt no need to get up, no desire to do anything but sit and reflect. I bowed my head until I felt a touch on my shoulder. I looked up. Carson stood in the aisle facing me. I rose and shook his hand.

"You must be Andre. Welcome, my friend."

I thanked him.

"So what did you think of the message this morning?" he asked.

It seemed, at first, an odd question, but he did not seem to need reassurance from my answer. The soft eyes and calm tone of his voice suggested that he was not a preacher who needed stroking. He asked the question because he really wanted to know what I thought of the sermon. I felt what it must have been like for Jesus to ask His disciples, "So who do you say that I am?" There was no arrogance to Carson's question and no hint that it might be misinterpreted as such.

"Deeply moving," I said. "Your message challenged me to the core of my soul, Pastor Carson."

Carson tilted his head slightly toward me as though what he wanted to say next was intended just for me. He stared hard, but his look was not intruding. "Milad shared with me briefly over the phone this morning that you're going through a very hard time. He did not tell me what but suggested I spend some time talking with you. Would you be willing to do that?"

Tears welled up in my eyes again. "Yes, Pastor, I would like that very much. I mean—I need—yes. Please, would you meet with me? I'm at the end of myself and need help." I choked up, fighting back another outpouring.

"I'm free tomorrow." Carson said. "Tell you what. Let me pick you up at Milad's in the morning. I've got a friend who owns a coffee shop down at Lake Michigan. We'll grab some coffee and have all day to talk. You'll love the view. We could even walk near the beach. Deal?"

“I’d really like that, Pastor. Thanks so much.”

As Carson spoke to a few more people, I stood near Milad while he talked with an Iranian couple. In no mood for conversation, I politely acknowledged Milad’s friends after being introduced. A half hour later, we headed back to Milad’s home. After parking, Pouri ran ahead of us. Jamileh walked a few paces behind Milad and me. As we entered the gate and approached the steps leading up to their home, I told Milad of Carson’s offer to meet the next day.

Milad stopped and faced me with a huge smile. “Wonderful, Andre. I'm so pleased. We know it’ll be good for you.” He grabbed my arms and pulled me into a strong hug. “Come in, my friend. Let’s eat and then you rest up as long as you need.”

Chapter 24

The next morning, Carson called to tell me he would arrive in twenty minutes. We drove forty minutes through Chicago. Finally, Carson pulled his car into a parking lot reserved for the patrons of the Water Front Café. A large sign near the path leading to the front door read, "A Dog-Friendly Seasonal Outdoor Café." We got out of the car. Carson hit the lock button on his remote. He laughed as an energetic boxer pulled away from his owner and ran toward us. Carson dropped to his knees, extending his arms to welcome the attack.

"Hey there, Pluto, you wild beast." The dog nearly knocked Carson over. Carson rubbed his hands across the dog's huge jowls. "Good boy, Pluto. That's it, you monster. Now, where's that cruel owner of yours? Is she around? Huh, boy? Where is she?"

"Pluto, stop. Leave Carson alone." A young woman rushed from the side of the Water Front Café to where we stood. Glancing at Carson, she leaned to the ground and picked up the dog's leash. Pluto obeyed the yanking of the leash, allowing Carson to stand.

"There she is. Hey, Steph. Thanks for rescuing me. I thought he'd eat me alive."

The woman laughed in a carefree way that would melt any man's heart. I felt guilty for the thought and fought off the stirring in my heart at noticing an attractive woman. Carson took several steps in her direction, embracing her. The woman, I noted, was both beautiful and sophisticated, much of what I expected in this section of Chicago. She wore white jeans and a light blue shirt. Her long blond hair moved lightly in the lake breeze. As she laughed again, she pushed back hair blown across her face by the wind.

"It is so good to see you, Steph. You doing well?" Carson's hand lingered on her shoulder for a few seconds as he pulled away from the hug.

"Sure am. And it's good to see you too, handsome. I thought you'd never come back."

Carson smiled.

"You promised we'd continue our discussion over that book you recommended I read. Remember?" She chuckled, slapped him lightly on his shoulder and then looked to me. "And who's this good-looking guy?"

This time the stirrings were harder to push away, but thankfully Carson intervened. "Meet my new friend, Andre. I told him about your place and suggested we come down here and spend a couple hours here. And yes, I thought this week that we need to get together. I'll call you in a few days, for sure."

"Great! I have lots of questions." Stephanie, laughing again, moved the leash to her left hand and extended her right hand to shake mine. Her eyes sparkled blue, like Sophia's, and soft lines highlighted her cheekbones. I felt like a teenager meeting a girl for the first time. Composing myself, I shook her hand. The soft skin and lingering grip momentarily distracted me from my longings for Sophia.

She removed her hand slowly. "Good to meet you, Andre. Stephanie Molyneux. It's such a pleasure. Any friend of Carson's is certainly going to be a friend of mine."

I looked at Carson, noticing the twinkle in his eyes along with a knowing look, as though he acknowledged both my discomfort and enjoyment in meeting Stephanie. "Steph owns this place, and it's the best hangout in Chicago."

"Well, don't just stand there. Come on in, boys." She waved us toward the café while leading Pluto that way, too. "I believe you're early enough to get the best view of the lake."

Adjacent to the café stood a fenced-off patch of grass. A sign to the left read, "Pet Relief Center." Stephanie closed the gate behind Pluto who ran excitedly toward another dog. When we entered the café, the smell of coffee blended with the outside smells of Lake Michigan, bringing back memories of living in Chicago and visiting the lake.

I looked around the half-filled room. There was something so familiar about this place. Then I remembered that Sophia and I had come to this café once for a getaway from the busyness of life at the food bank. That meant we'd come to Berger Park, which included a community garden and a beautiful walking path on the edge of one of Chicago's best beaches. A warm breeze filtered through the open windows of the café. Stephanie took us to a table in a semi-private corner with a stunning view of the lake and the wooded park to our left.

"When you guys know what you want, just wave over to the bar. If I'm busy, Sarah will get your order. And Carson, call me some time, okay? Let's catch up. I've taken some art classes, and I'm dying to show you some of my work. You'll love it."

Carson smiled. When Stephanie walked away, he looked at me. "She's really a great gal. Probably one of the most intelligent women I have ever known. She's gone through a lot and has been pretty open about those things the last few times we've met." Carson left me to wonder if perhaps the two had an interest in each other as he picked up a menu. "The best thing here is their vanilla milkshake. Best in Chicago. Tell me what you want, and we'll order. Then we can talk."

Carson waved to Sarah. I ordered a bold Sumatra coffee while he ordered the vanilla milkshake. Five minutes later, Sarah returned with our drinks. We made small talk for a while. Carson did not seem rushed either with his milkshake or to enter into deep conversation with me about my situation. I decided to take the initiative.

As I had when I recounted the story to Milad, I wept and did not care when others in the café looked in my direction. Neither did Carson mind. He seemed to invite it. Several times he touched my arm, squeezed it for a moment, and said, "Don't hold back, brother," or "Jesus cares very deeply for you right now."

When I completed my story—and I mean all of it, from the accusations to my obsession to kill the man who took Priscilla's life—Carson surprised me by saying very little. "May I ask you a question?" I said.

"You just did," Carson replied with a clever smile. "What's your next one?"

We both laughed. It was good to have someone to be lighthearted with.

"You mentioned yesterday that Jesus was settled with himself, that His two natures, God and man, did not conflict but worked together."

Carson looked at me with gentle eyes, comforting me. He sipped his drink slowly, waiting to hear more. I appreciated someone who would not rush me.

"I look at Jesus and how He lived this un-conflicted life, but as much as I have preached on it and worshiped because of it, I have never seen how it addresses the conflict between my two natures. Even with Paul's depiction of this wrestling between his two natures and his conclusion that Jesus rescues him from his wretchedness, I've never understood how this helps us, other than to say, 'Yup, I like Paul. He struggled just like I do.' I relate more to Paul's struggle, though, than to his conclusion of victory in Jesus."

Carson held up his right index finger. "You're asking if it is possible to live the un-conflicted life Jesus lived, or was His life something that was unique to Him because He was both God and man?"

"Yes," I said, "That's a fair way to put it."

Carson nodded. He took a quick sip from his milkshake, the gurgling reminding me of Priscilla laughing at the sound as she sucked hard through her straw. "Since Jesus was God and man but lived in reliance not on His God-ness but on His humanity, can humans live as He did?"

"Absolutely," I answered. "But this is not a theological dilemma to me. It's at the heart of my struggle. I have lived a fleshly life, an angry life, under the cover of a pastor. I did the church thing but moonlighted as a sinner, and I realize now—and I mean this—that I am a sinner. A wretched, confused person who had refused to be rescued. I don't know how to be rescued. I feel trapped. Oh sure, I felt some release yesterday after attending church, and I sensed some relief that I failed to kill a man the other day, but those are circumstantial things. They have not changed who I am." Describing myself in this way filled my eyes with tears. I struggled to speak, so Carson continued for me.

"You fear that when you leave here, you will find yourself as angry as you were when you arrived."

"Yes," I said, resigned.

Several people left the café, making it easier to talk. The more I spoke with Carson, the more choked up I became. My voice shook. "I'm so afraid. Not afraid of what to go back to or where I should go, I'm afraid of what exists inside me."

I paused for what seemed an eternity. I knew what I said next could volley the final blow against that lifelong dam I had built. "I know deep in my heart that Priscilla's and Sophia's deaths destroyed me. Like the author of Hebrews wrote, 'I am laid bare before Him to whom I must give an account.' I used to think if I faced a tragedy, I'd be strong and able to withstand it. Yet each crisis, first Priscilla, then the accusations, then Sophia's death, worked like huge claws, tearing away thick layers of my soul and each stripping made me more afraid of what I'd discover about myself." My volume rose with each word until I was nearly screaming. I did not care when several heads at the bar turned my direction. "I feel I'm dying but a different kind of dying. Help me!"

I flung my arms open, then brought my hands in and pounded lightly at my chest. "Something spiritual in me is dying, and it's agonizing!"

Carson again put his hand on my arm. "You need to experience that death. You need to embrace it, accept it, and discover something there that will turn your life upside down."

I never met anyone so patient. I was certainly not like him when counseling others. I was Mr. Quick Fix. Share your problem with me, brother, and here you go: 1–2–3. Try it, and call me in the morning. I noticed a slight smile on Carson's face as though he read right through my last vestige of cynicism. I nodded for him to continue.

"Here's my question: what do you think God wants to do for you right now?"

I paused for a long time, staring at the old brick that made up the inside of this café, noting a style similar to that of the church where I met Carson the day before. "I really don't know," I said. "I feel so far from Him. I can't even begin to answer that question because I've lost touch with Him."

I lowered my head, feeling the shame of thinking I could ever really run from God. "I ran to get away from my problems and to get away from Him." Embarrassed, I could only stare at the bottom of my empty coffee mug. The cup seemed as empty as my life right now. I looked back up at Carson. "Are you married?" I had been curious about this since I met him.

"I was," he replied with a little discomfort.

"Have children?"

"I did," he replied reluctantly.

"What happened to them?" I persisted.

"They were taken from me." Carson shifted. "If you knew my story, you wouldn't believe it. And if I told you my history now, it might distract from what God wants to show you."

Not wanting to push this, I returned to our previous discussion. "What do I do now, Carson? How do I move on? Right now, I feel safe. I feel secure with you. But I'm telling you," my voice shook again with emotion, "I can't move from here until I know I can walk out those doors and not become hateful again. I'm scared."

Carson's gaze unsettled me. When he spoke, a slight twinkle rose in his eye. "The hour has come for you to wake up from your slumber, bro. Because your salvation is nearer than you think."

I considered this for a few seconds. "Wait a minute," I exclaimed, "Paul wrote that in Romans."

"Yes, he sure did. And it's still true, my friend!" Carson placed his elbows on the table, leaned forward, and lowered his voice. "I can tell you one thing and then it's up to you to walk out of here and put it into practice. This will not sound very profound, but it's what saved me. It's what keeps me going today."

"I'm ready. Give it to me."

Carson scooted his chair closer to the table. "You're misguided in thinking that somehow you can live for God and manage your anger. Don't think that Jesus lived free of unrighteous anger, and we cannot."

He paused while a young couple walked past our table. The couple, infatuated, stopped just two feet from us and faced each other. The two stared longingly. Just as they began to lean together for a kiss, Carson said, "Hey, you two." Startled, the couple noticed us. "I'm not sure if this will help, but I'm a pastor, and I can perform a wedding ceremony right here, right now." The enamored couple laughed and walked toward the door without kissing each other.

Carson chuckled. He leaned back and said nothing until the couple had left the café. I found myself staring after them with a longing for Sophia that increased the ache in my heart.

His voice grew serious again. "Listen, people struggle between two natures and mistakenly think they need to discard one for the other. But the beauty of regeneration is that God consumes us with Himself instead of replacing us with something else. He takes our whole being, now fully His, and immerses it in His love and character. You remember yesterday I spoke of how Jesus, being both God and man, was comfortable with this and never in conflict?"

"Sure, I remember," I said. "It's how we started this conversation."

"Of course. It's what the resurrection is all about. When Paul said, 'I have been crucified with Christ, and it is no longer I who live, but Christ who lives in me,' he did not mean that the you that made up you disappears. Rather, that you—your flesh and your soul along with your emotions and personality, everything that defines you now—belong to Jesus. Not discarded but transformed. God living in man does not need to create a conflict."

"What about what Paul wrote," I interrupted, "about his battle between his two natures? Did he not suggest that there will always be conflict in us? It's all I've ever known."

Carson tried another sip from his straw only to find the cup empty. Disappointed, he leaned to his left and tossed it into a nearby garbage can. Taking a napkin, he wiped the table and spoke again. "Let's go outside and take a walk along the beach. You will love it, and we can take all the time we need to talk this over."

The small light, which hung over our table and gave off a soft glow, flickered a few times. Carson smiled. "That happens a lot here. It's an old building. More reason for us to go outside."

Carson stood, and after paying, he looked around the room. Then he walked to the bar and asked Sarah for a couple of waters to go, but I wondered if his real motive was to look for Stephanie. She was nowhere to be seen, so we made our way to the door. I opened the door for Carson who held the two plastic glasses of water.

"Hey, Carson," a voice called. "Just a minute." Both of us stopped and turned to the voice. "Don't you dare leave before giving your good friend Steph a big hug." Stephanie walked toward us. "And I might even give one to handsome here, too."

Carson handed me my glass of water as Stephanie hugged him, but her eyes fixed on me. I felt disarmed but also warmed. Carson laughed as Stephanie threw her arms around my shoulders. Not sure how to respond, I placed my left arm around her and patted her back several times before pulling away. "Sure good to meet you, Stephanie," I said. "You've got a great place here. I'm sure we'll return."

"You better, big guy." She punched me on the shoulder and pointed at Carson. "Even if this guy doesn't come with you, you're welcome on your own." She winked at me as we stepped outside.

The back door of The Water Front Café brought us to a small porch with four lampposts at each corner. Carson pushed a small gate and stepped onto a path made of large, flat stones and surrounded by carefully manicured grass, similar to what you would see on a golf course. We joined several others on the paved walk that ran alongside the beach. It was a warm day, and many in Chicago were taking advantage of it.

A mother pushing a stroller moved to the side, allowing us to pass. I smiled at the sight of the toddler, sound asleep, oblivious to the beautiful surroundings. Carson passed a hand through his hair, adjusting the band holding his ponytail. I wondered if Sophia would have allowed me to grow my hair to that length. I smiled as I imagined her response.

Two girls jogging toward us slowed their pace to nearly a walk to pass us. Both looked at us, and I wondered what they thought. Sophia often commented in a jealous and protective way that women looked at me far too long for her comfort. I shrugged off the thoughts and feelings that struggled for my attention. Carson and I had far greater things to discuss.

Picking up his pace, Carson spoke first. "Okay, where were we?"

"I was telling you how all I know is this conflict between my two natures."

"Oh, yes."

We walked a few more paces before Carson continued. "When Paul talked about his struggle between two natures, don't forget that in the end he exclaimed that his victory rested in Jesus and what He had accomplished for Paul. Paul celebrated that the struggle was resolved at the cross and with the resurrection of Jesus. Paul understood with his mind that the battle ended at the cross. The discipline for Paul was inviting his whole being into the reality of this change."

"Man, that's good stuff. Keep going."

"You see, like Jesus, we can also be comfortable in our own skins. This state of being was not unique to Jesus. What pleases God is not that we get rid of who we are but that we commit who we are to His purposes."

Carson slowed his pace and lifted the plastic glass of water in his hands. "Take this glass of water, for example. The glass represents me or rather, my outward man. The water represents the content of my life."

He stopped and faced me, holding the glass up between us. I saw his distorted face through the water. Carson lowered the glass to chest level, and we resumed our walk. "Before Christ, this glass was corrupt with sin because of what's inside. Jesus, through His death in my place, which satisfied the wrath of God placed on me, has been given the right, by His Father, to turn the glass upside down. It's my being crucified with Him, my burial, and then turning my life right side up again and filling me with Himself."

Carson sipped from the glass, and we both laughed. "Sorry," he said, feigning embarrassment. "Had to. I was thirsty. It's hot out here."

We walked a few more paces before saying anything. I was relaxed and enjoying this moment but knew I had so much more to work through. I saw a small rock on the path and scooted it mindlessly with my foot. The rock landed in front of Carson. He kicked it back in my direction and chuckled.

"Should we see how far we can keep this going?"
"Sure," I teased, but my next attempt put the rock out of both our reaches.

"Okay, back to my object lesson," Carson resumed. "Just like a glass doesn't change when you put something new in it, neither do we. The glass does not change but instead becomes transformed by the content inside. You remember that Paul said, 'If anyone is in Christ, he is a new creation; the old is gone, but the new has come.' The old and new that he talks about is not our body but the spirit in us. When a person comes to Jesus, he or she doesn't receive a new body, right?"

"That's right," I answered.

"Rather, he now has the opportunity to allow this body, for the days left on Earth, to be a vessel completely available to the Creator. One day, that body will die and be buried but not discarded. It'll be resurrected again. The same body you live with and don't like because it is aging will be your perfect body for eternity. Just as Jesus' body was buried and the same body rose to new life. These bodies, Andre, matter to God."

I smiled and decided to tell him of the moment when Priscilla became a follower of Jesus at the age of four. We were visiting Sophia's sister, Rachel, in northern California, and one night during supper, Priscilla begged to pray for the meal. She uttered the usual things, thanking Jesus for the food and all that, and then suddenly to our surprise, she said, "And Jesus, please come into my life, and forgive me of my sins."

We all laughed and cried together.

"Do you know what I did?" I said.

"Give it to me!" Carson exclaimed.

"Well, I immediately took the glass she had been drinking from, grabbed her hand, and walked outside while the others remained at the table. I found a faucet on the back side of the house and sat her down and explained to her pretty much what you're telling me now. I took her glass full of water and filled it up with dirt from near our feet. I explained that her life before that night was like this glass, but during supper, she understood what Jesus did for her at the cross, and by her faith through that prayer, it became her experience. Jesus took the glass and like you said, He did not break it and replace it but took that same body, emptied it of sin, and replaced it with something new: Himself. 'Now Jesus lives in you, Priscilla. You get to live for Jesus,' I remember shouting out with joy."

As I recounted this story, tears filled my eyes, and when they cleared enough, I saw Carson's eyes held tears, too. I wondered again what memories stirred over his loss while I talked.

Carson apparently pushed away his own feelings. "I can't say much more, Andre, except this. Are you ready?"

"Still am," I said, smiling broadly.

We walked a few more paces, then Carson turned to face the lake. I joined him, noticing again how blue the water was. Several gulls swooped low over the lake. A sail boat moved slowly across the horizon. A hand grabbed my shoulder. I looked at Carson. He lifted his other arm and pointed out to the ocean-like expanse of water in front of us. "Go, young man. Go and live for Jesus. Stop struggling." Carson turned to me, placing both hands on my shoulders. "God lives in you." He used his index finger to tap on my chest. "And He's brought you to the end of yourself, so you would have no struggle left. So He could finally claim you, Andre. All of you. Body, soul, and spirit. For Himself. Go, and live for Him."

We began walking slowly again. He grew very serious. "But Andre, it'll very likely be hard because He'll ask you to do something He asked of me."

"Okay." I said eagerly.

"To live for Jesus means you must love like Jesus. Just like anger needs an object to hate, love needs an object to love. In Romans, Paul referred to it as the continued debt of love. 'Love,' Paul also said, 'is the requirement of the law.' You owe Jesus something. Do you know what it is?"

My eyes stung from the remnants of tears pushing for release. Yes, I knew. To end this conflict, love must replace hate. Hate had looked for its object. I failed miserably as its custodian. Something stirred in me. The open space around us grew small, as though Carson and I were the only ones there. Eventually, he disappeared as well. The desire to love overwhelmed me, and I let go of hate.

God's love overwhelmed me. I wanted to laugh. I had never felt this kind of love. I could not explain it. It started in what had to be the deep seat of my being, my spirit, rushing past my soul, and impacting everything in me. I felt my broken heart mended by invisible hands. I felt a surge of joy that was emotional, spiritual, and physical all at once. I was being invaded. All I could see was the freshness of blue water before me. I felt a cleansing torrent sweeping away the pain, the anger, the fear, and the doubt. My hands opened. Warm, refreshing air joined another movement that filled me with a joy I had never experienced before. My head rose. I shouted. I'm not sure what I said, but I shouted. I cried out to God. I thanked Him. I praised Him. Every fiber in my soul responded to what I knew to be one thing and one thing only. It had pursued me. It had found me.

I looked up at my new friend. "Carson, I've heard His Whisper. He's been speaking to me all this time, and my life, this stubbornness of my life, blocked him out. I've ignored His voice clearly heard in scripture, and now for the first time, really for the first time, I can hear him."

Tears spilled from his eyes. "Yes, my friend, you have. Indeed, you have."

Chapter 25

Carson and I spent many hours together in the three weeks I remained in Chicago. I also experienced the joy of meeting and spending some time with Sami's wife, Mehrnoosh, and their four-year-old son, Ahmed. I ate many meals with Milad and Jamileh and loved playing chess with Pouri. Yes, the girl loved chess and was very good at it.

The prayers, admonitions, and urgings of Milad and Carson led me to decide to travel back to Lowensville. I did not feel I had to. I wanted to. I knew trials would challenge my new faith but love drove me. A love I knew would lead me to two men I once hated. And while I knew the men who took Sophia's life must pay for their crimes, I longed for them to know what it meant to be loved. I longed to give them that love. If hate needed an object so did love. Love drove me to offer forgiveness. Living the debt of love allowed me to live as one man, un-conflicted and undeterred. Love allowed me to trust God and not feel the need to trust people. I believe Dr. Sommeral wanted to tell me this earlier, but he knew I was not ready to hear the answer then.

I remembered his accent now. "Yes, Andre, you can trust God when you no longer trust people because God is trustworthy. You need no other reason to trust."

# # #

Life back in Lowensville is marked by suspicion. Few trust me. I am nervous but also eager to face them. I know I have a long road ahead of me. Rumors of a pastor gone rogue give women in hair salons and men in bars enough gossip to keep themselves busy for hours. News of the upcoming trial consumes the local papers. Even some of the regional media outlets begin to speak about it. I try to settle back as I wait.

Only Dr. Sommeral feels at ease around me. We meet almost daily. Today he tells me that the elders have spoken to him and want to meet with me soon. "The men are shattered by what happened, Andre," he explains. "They need to talk to you. Give them a few weeks, though. I think Ned is digging his heels, and they want to make sure he's on board before you meet with them."

Later, my phone rings as I am standing in front of my stove, a piece of chicken just beginning to sizzle in grease. I turn the stove off and move the pan to a back burner. Leaning across the counter, I grab the phone.

"Hello," I untie the strings of my apron.

"Simeon here, Andre. Welcome home."

Cradling the phone with my chin and shoulder, I lift the apron over my head, nearly losing my grip on the phone but managing to place the apron on the dining room chair. "Thank you. You know, it's actually good to be home."

"You sound relaxed. Where did you go?"

"Chicago. And yes, I feel good. A lot happened there. I'll explain someday. So, what have you got for me, Simeon? News of the trial?"

"Yes. The trial is scheduled to begin in three weeks. August 18th."

"Where?" I ask nervously.

"Well, that's the thing. The judge decided to hold it in Lowensville after all. According to the judge, we would have had to move it to another state to get far enough away from people who know the details and from people who have been influenced by Whitlock Larson in one way or other. "

The calmness in my voice surprises me. "I guess that makes sense."

"So anyway, let's get together on Wednesday and begin reviewing your testimony. We'll go over details of the case. Should be cut and dry."

I thank Simeon, hang up the phone, place my head in my palms, and find the desire to pray stronger than ever before. Twin emotions—love and anger—jostle for position in my heart, but love is weakening anger. Anger's grip loosens its hold, attached now by only a few hateful strands. I know the Holy Spirit is doing something I could not do in my own strength. I think of Whitlock and find myself praying for him even as the scenes in my living room, of Cleon's gun pointing at me, then at Sophia, play in mind.

Chapter 26

Long after dark on the night before the trail begins, a knock sounds at my door. Three of the four elders from the church stand sheepishly on my porch. The harshness of the memory of having my feet washed by these men, followed by their request that I resign, diminishes at the realization that I love them. I invite them in.

George pauses in the hallway. "Ned's not coming. He just couldn't face you, we think. We invited him, but he..."

I put my hand on George's shoulder. "It's really okay. I'm fine." I motion to Jim and Nicholas to take a seat on the couch, while I sit on the recliner. George settles in the armchair next to me. I look at each man and sigh. "Before you all say anything, I want to start by saying I hold nothing against you. The Lord has taken me through a journey of deep brokenness these past couple of months, and I need to tell you I'm a free man. Free from anger and free from hate."

A look of relief settles across the face of each man. Jim speaks up first, his voice shaking with emotion. "Thank you for that, Pastor. Thank you so much." His head lowers, and he begins to sob.

Nicholas takes up the conversation. "Pastor, we were wrong. We were so wrong to be suspicious of you. And we were wrong to act so quickly in urging you to resign. It was such a confusing time for us, and besides that…"

"Guys." I hold up my hands. "I embrace your coming here as an act of repentance and sorrow. I forgive you. Each of you. There is no need to say more."

I move to Jim. He stands. We hug. He sobs, and I join him. Another arm reaches across mine. Then another. The four of us stand in my living room, arms locked around each other. When we pull back, our arms remain latched on to each other's shoulders.

"We will be at the trial tomorrow to support you," Nicholas says.

"Thank you." Tears stream down my face, but I refuse to use my hand to wipe them away because doing so would mean letting go of my hold on the men standing next to me. George laughs as he reaches a hand toward his pocket. He pulls out a handkerchief and wipes my cheek for me. I smile.

George stuffs the wet handkerchief back in his pocket. "Men, let's pray for our pastor."

We bow our heads, the four of us locked in a new commitment, experiencing a new love, one that replaces all the hurt we experienced together. As George prays, I open my eyes and realize our small circle of restoration covers the very spot where Sophia died.

The last strand holding on to hate snaps. The final splinter of rage dies. I feel an overwhelming sense of peace. The very place where Sophia left me becomes my place of renewed hope.

Chapter 27

I wake up the morning of Whitlock's trial unusually refreshed. Simeon and I have gone over detail after detail of the trial during these past three weeks. I might testify, but Simeon feels it will not come to that. He believes the trial will last only a week, followed shortly by Cleon's. There is too much evidence against Whitlock and Cleon for it to drag on forever, especially since Cleon has been talking non-stop. Everything he offers matches perfectly with details of the investigation, especially my testimony.

Any minute, Dr. Sommeral will arrive. Outside, it's warm and appears muggy. The weatherman predicts temperatures will reach 85 degrees today, with 70 percent humidity. A bead of sweat finds its way down the large line of my forehead. I intercept it, sigh, and for the tenth time in five minutes look out the window. Dr. Sommeral should be here by now.

Finally, dust clouds spray from the back tires of the familiar Volvo rambling up my gravel road. I grab my wallet and rush to the door. Then I stop. For the first time since last night, I look around the living room. Heavy breathing fills the silence.

The breathing is mine. It stops for a few seconds then returns. That place, that spot, no longer holds the stains of hate.

I push away the emotion and move toward the door again. Dr. Sommeral, predictably patient, stands at the front of his car, waiting. We hug. The motor hums while I move toward the passenger seat. Dr. Sommeral takes his place behind the wheel. We drive down the driveway, pass the pond I built for Sophia, and exit onto the main road toward town. I feel no need to speak. Neither does the doctor.

The courthouse looms large over the center of Lowensville. The clock tower chimes 2 o'clock as we approach the only parking place available. The moment I open my door, a microphone appears in front of my face. Behind the reporter, dozens of others press toward us.

"Mr. Lansing!" a voice screams out. "Do you want Whitlock Larson and Cleon Lewis sent to the gas chamber for murdering your wife?"

"No comment," I say, obeying Simeon's instructions.

"But Pastor Lansing," another reporter shouts. "They murdered your wife. Surely you want them…"

I hear nothing more as I push my way out of the car and then through the growing crowd. Dr. Sommeral calmly presses on ahead of me, like Moses paving a way through the Red Sea. Instead of stepping into the Promised Land, we stumble into the hallway of the courthouse.

A security officer approaches. "Mr. Lansing, please come this way."

I follow him to the elevator.

"This'll take us to the fourth floor," the guard explains. "It's the best way to avoid all those dang reporters. You too, Dr. Sommeral. Right this way."

I thank the security guard as the three of us stand in the enclosure of the elevator. The numbers slowly increase. At the third floor, my heart begins to pound. All this—the reporters outside, the selection of the jury, the choice of the judge—all this because of Sophia. The death of my Sophia.

I cannot shake off the tragedy. Even in my willingness to offer forgiveness, I will not and cannot minimize the horror of what took place. It began with the accusation of sexual advances toward Whitlock's wife and ended with Sophia's tragic death. Or did it end with my death? A man who lost his reputation and also lost the love of his life. Yet this tragedy also included the rescue of that man's soul. My soul.

I am about to face the man who took away my soul mate. Most around me want him to die. I, too, want him to die. But I desire a different kind of death for him. I want him to discover what I discovered, that life that can only come by way of death.

I can do this because several weeks ago I met the Man who made my own death possible, the Man who invited me to discover new life through His death and resurrection.

Who dies not before he dies is ruined when he dies.

—German mystic Jakob Böhme

AUTHOR'S NOTE

A good portion of this book mirrors my own story. What is reflected will not necessarily be clear to others. Few, except for my family and several close friends, will directly connect what I write to specific events in my life. Even some of those that know, after reading the draft, wondered if I had written about situations familiar to them. I enjoyed leaving them wondering! The purpose of this book is not to dissect my personal events but rather use them to tell a bigger story. I wanted this story to play out what it would look like for a man under accusation to rebel against God. If we all paused long enough to consider the consequences of our response to abuse, accusations, or trials, we might make better choices. That is what I am hoping for.

I concluded that much of what happens to us is meant for us. Believing this lessens my resistance. What I mean is this: the people God puts in our path and the troubles they sometimes place on us become God's way of stripping us so that we are left defenseless, and He can do His best work. It took Jonah running from God for him to run into God. Even our rebellion is sometimes the path God uses to bring us home.

Andre Michael Lansing, like Jonah, learned a hard lesson that might benefit the reader of this story. You can't run from God. Hold on, though, because sometimes our trying to run is what it takes for us to truly meet Him, to come to the place where, perhaps for the first time, your soul is completely quiet, and you can hear His whisper. His whisper is heard through the scriptures. I am convinced of that. One popular speaker often says, "If you want to hear God speak, open your Bible. If you want to hear God speak audibly, read your Bible out loud." His Word, what we know as Holy Scripture, is the way God speaks. Through these years, as my life has quieted from the loud noises around me, what He has to say to me as I immerse myself in His word is so wonderful, so clean, so holy, so good.

As is true for most of us, it is impossible to pinpoint the exact moment Andre Michael Lansing experienced his spiritual restoration. Andre's transformation was a process that occurred progressively through his brokenness.

When we embrace this concept that we also are never changed in just one moment, we discover that transformation is both underlying and potent. There is a sense that this transformation is not just indescribable but is, in every sense, wonderfully mysterious.

The mystery that exists for all of us is to understand exactly what happens when God finally grabs hold of our lives. Did God allow Andre to experience tragedy as part of his transformation? If so, were Sophia's and Priscilla's deaths really senseless? Or were these losses necessary as God's way of rescuing Andre?

I leave the story where I do so that you, the reader, will question not just how Andre got here. but what he does next. (Of course, you have the opportunity to read more in my sequel to this story, *The Guardians*, now available on Amazon.) At the risk of comparing my novel to the Bible's story of Jonah, I want you to wonder and by wondering, identify better with the character. When we question why Jonah's story ends the way it does, it moves the attention from his story to our own. Left wondering what happened next to Jonah (and Andre), we begin to mull over what is next for us.

So what is next for you?

There is only one way to be free of anger and that is to embrace the love of Jesus.

Many people try to manage life on their own. Some struggle to deal with loss and injustice through their own effort. As with Andre, choosing this path leads to personal chaos. During this life, people will do things to you that produce bitterness and anger. Trying to manage these feelings on your own will lead to greater difficulty and pain.

There is another option. In fact, there is only one other option, and it leads to freedom.

None of us have a right to hold on to anger. The Bible makes it very clear that only God holds the responsibility to carry out judgment on those who have done wrong or on behalf of those who have been wronged. We have all done wrong; therefore, we are all under the condemnation of God. I was born with a nature that is sick and damaged by sin. So were you. We inherited this condition from our first parents, Adam and Eve, and it defines us. When we are wronged, we must first remember that we also do wrong. Mainly, we have wronged God.

We do wrong because there is something inherently wrong with us. Until we hang on a cross despite having been perfectly righteous, we have no right to ever hold anger toward others. Only Jesus holds that right. And because Jesus lived a perfect life and died a perfect death in our place even though we were the ones who deserved death, God withdrew His judgment from us. It was all placed instead on His perfect Son, Jesus. Accepting what Jesus did in your place, admitting that your condition is sick and damaged by sin, and seeking His love and forgiveness is what God longs for you (and all of us) to do. It is the only way to live a free and full life. The acknowledgement of Jesus' death and admission of our need because of sin become the door to what we call salvation. That is, God reaches out and saves us through Jesus. Then He transforms us through a life-long process of change. The model for this change is the perfect life of Jesus.

Our anger, lack of trust, and doubt all expose a heart that has yet to capture the beauty of salvation that God extends to us through Jesus. Andre took a long time and walked a hard path before he discovered this. His wife, Sophia, lived it. If you are angry toward someone, or angry at God, this anger might be the Holy Spirit reminding you of your need for forgiveness. The best way to capture what Jesus did in dying on the cross is to let go of anger, forgive those who have wronged you, and let Him replace your hatred with love. There is something about acting on this toward others that shows us so much more clearly what God did for us.

I would love to hear from you, especially if you have come to this crisis place of need to embrace Jesus and His forgiveness. Perhaps you need someone to talk to about this. We want to be there for you. You may contact me at:
mitchschultz@me.com

Discussion Questions for The Whisper

INTRODUCTION:

Overview:

The book was written to play out what it looks like to choose rebellion over obedience. I have been obedient in the sufferings of my life, but I don't think I have appreciated their true value. I needed to know what it would have looked like if I had not trusted Jesus because of the suffering I went through. Thus the book.

Questions:

Why is obedience in suffering so important? Reflect on Jesus being obedient to death in Phil. 2:8. Discuss together what your life would be like had you not trusted Jesus. How would things have been different for Andre if he had trusted and obeyed Jesus in all that he suffered?

SECTION ONE - FEAR:

Overview:

Andre is falsely accused, and it devastates him. He is afraid and realizes that everything in his life hangs by a thread. He meets a man dying in the hospital who speaks to him about the importance of fear. Prov. 1:7 speaks of fear being the beginning of wisdom. In Gen. 31:42, God is referred to as the Fear of Isaac. Andre's fear unsettles him. He finds himself losing control. As with Jonah, fear ends up being good for Andre.

Questions:

1. Discuss together what fear has looked like in your life. Give it a name. What have you been afraid of? What are you afraid of now? (Example: A mom fears that she will lose her teenage daughter.)
2. What is healthy about fear?
3. When does it become unhealthy?
4. Why does God allow us to fear?
5. What would the absence of fear look like?

SECTION TWO - ANGER:

Overview:

Andre goes back to Lowensville, and his life falls apart. His elders seem to reject him. We also discover in this section the details of his daughter's tragic death which serves as the backdrop to how Andre and Sophia ended up in Lowensville. The only man Andre trusts is Dr. Sommeral. Dr. Sommeral says to Andre that his anger is ultimately directed at God.

Questions:

1. Read Gen. 4:6-7 and discuss what happens when you do not harness anger.
2. Why is it easier to blame God rather than people for our misfortunes?
3. What would it have taken for Andre to manage his anger?
4. Andre finds that those close to him pull away when the accusation becomes known. Why do we find it hard to support those who are suffering injustice? What do you risk when you come alongside someone who might even be guilty of sin?
5. What could the elders of Andre's church have done to better trust and care for their pastor?
6. How supportive is your church of the pastors who shepherd you?

SECTION THREE - DOUBT

Overview:

Andre loses control. The elders reject him, and his best friends pull away. Then his wife is brutally murdered. Who can blame Andre for being angry? In his anger, however, Andre rejects the Church and turns his back on God.

Questions:

1. Andre asks Dr. Sommeral, "Can you still trust God when you have lost your trust in people?" How would you answer that question?
2. If you suddenly had everything taken from you, how would you respond? What would it do to your faith?
3. Share with each other what tragedies/difficulties have done to your walk with Jesus.
4. Andre discovers in Sophia's journal that she harbored but overcame the desire to seek revenge for the death of their daughter, Priscilla. Love overwhelmed her, not hate. What has that tension between hate and love looked like in your life? How would your journal read?

SECTION FOUR - TRUST

Overview:

Andre leaves for Chicago bent on taking the life of the man who took the life of his daughter. He leaves behind him all the principles that had previously driven his life. In Chicago, he meets a family who impresses him with their simple faith and trust in Jesus. His obsession to kill the object of his hate leads to frustration when he discovers the young man took his own life several years before. The Iranian family takes Andre to church where he meets Carson, the pastor. Carson speaks a new hope and a new faith into Andre's life, one that pushes Andre to his knees where he finally meets Jesus.

Questions:

1. What did Andre hope to accomplish by taking the life of the young man? What does this teach you about the futility of your anger toward others?
2. Carson speaks of Jesus "being comfortable in His own skin." By this, he meant that Jesus showed us how, with His help, we can also live free of the conflict between hate and love. How did this conversation encourage you and give you hope in your struggle between your two natures?
3. Andre's final breaking and victory came with the prayer, "Oh, God. I understand now. You allowed Priscilla to die. You took Sophia from me. You permitted the accusations. And in Your mystery and sovereignty, You used all these as certain and final blows to cause my death."

   Many have written to me expressing their struggle with this conclusion. One of the luxuries of working out my own theology in the form of a novel is allowing the reader to figure out which beliefs belong to the author and which belong to the character in the book. In the end, I concede that this has been the conclusion of my own life. I would not be who I am today had God not taken my son through cancer. I would not be who I am today if my wife had not also suffered cancer resulting in a long-haul recovery time to regain her speech, reading, writing and cognitive abilities. I would not be who I am today had God not placed me in a severely unhealthy church.

   While I was never accused of the charges brought against Andre, the pressures against me were just as harsh and real as they were to him. The conclusion that God meant all this for me is also my conclusion. I own it! I would never dare conclude that for you. It is up to God to reveal Himself to the soul of the sufferer. This is simply my story—and yes, I am sticking to it.

Discuss together what this story does to your own theology of suffering.

4. In light of your theology of suffering, how does the suffering of Jesus, His death and resurrection and ascension, serve as the basis for making sense of your trials?

I would love to interact with you directly about any thoughts or questions you might have. Feel free to write me at: mitchschultz@me.com

You can now order all three books in the Andre Michael Lansing series by going to www.amazon.com

BOOK TWO - THE GUARDIANS

Was Carson wrong to marry Gentiva? From the moment he took his first pastorate in the mountains of North Carolina, he remained resolute in his commitment.

Betrayed and unknowingly the subject of a madman's (The Whisper) obsession to seek revenge, Carson's world is held together only by the unconditional support of his elders (his guardians) and the relentless faithfulness of his Savior.

This story of innocence, betrayal, and near personal and spiritual collapse make it practically impossible to read this book in more than two sittings. In a surprising series of twists and turns, The Guardians *challenges many of the assumptions of what it really means to trust God through the people He places in our lives.*

BOOK THREE - THE CLAIM

How much more can a man take before he reaches his breaking point? *In this third and final installment of the Andre Michael Lansing series, we meet a troubled man, Liam Blythe. Some bad choices bring about tragedy at home and damage to his role as a shepherd to others. As if that's not enough, Liam faces the real prospect of losing one of his children to terminal cancer.*

The only thing Liam Blythe has left, aside from his sanity, is flying and flight Instructing. When that is nearly taken from him, his friend Andre steps in to help guide Liam to a new place of trust and devotion but in a way that would end up costing one of them dearly.

The Claim is a fast-paced, suspenseful story that will challenge you to a deeper and lasting trust and appreciation in the One who has his claim on your life.

Made in the USA
Columbia, SC
17 October 2022

69521440R00113